BEFORE SHE KILLS

THE FREDRIC BROWN PULP DETECTIVE SERIES

1. **HOMICIDE SANITARIUM**
2. **BEFORE SHE KILLS**
3. **MADMAN'S HOLIDAY**
4. **TCOT DANCING SANDWICHES**
5. **THE FREAK SHOW MURDERS**
6. **30 CORPSES EVERY THURSDAY**
7. **PARDON MY GHOULISH LAUGHTER**
8. **RED IS THE HUE OF HELL**
9. **BROTHER MONSTER**
10. **SEX LIFE ON THE PLANET MARS**

And, ..., more to come!

The **Fredric Brown Pulp Detective Series** presents the best of his previously uncollected work, plus some previously unpublished material, primarily in the mystery genre, but also including some sf and fantasy pieces.

BEFORE SHE KILLS

~

FREDRIC BROWN
in the
Detective Pulps
Volume 2

With a biographical introduction by
William F. Nolan

1984

BEFORE SHE KILLS (collection) © 1984 by
Elizabeth C. Brown.
All rights reserved.

"Introduction," copyright © 1984 by William F. Nolan.

"Before She Kills," *Ed McBain's Mystery Magazine No. 3,*
  copyright © 1961 by Pocket Books, Inc.
"The Missing Actor," *The Saint Detective Magazine,* November
  1963, copyright © 1963 by King Size Publications, Inc.
"Mad Dog!," *Detective Book Magazine,* Spring 1942, copyright
  © 1942, by Love Romances Publishing Co.
"A Date To Die," *Strange Detective Mysteries,* July 1942,
  copyright © 1942, copyright renewed 1970, by Popular
  Publications.
"A Cat Walks," *Detective Story Magazine,* April 1942, copyright
  © 1942, by Street & Smith Publications, Inc.
"Handbook for Homicide," *Detective Tales,* March 1942,
  copyright © 1942, copyright renewed 1970, by Popular
  Publications, Inc.

Cover design by William L. McMillan

First paperback edition published December 1986

Dennis McMillan Publications
1995 Calais Dr. No. 3
Miami Beach, FL 33141

CONTENTS

Introduction	5
A Date To Die	11
Mad Dog!	33
Handbook for Homicide	55
Before She Kills	101
A Cat Walks	137
The Missing Actor	163

INTRODUCTION

FRED BROWN REMEMBERED

by

William F. Nolan

A snapshot represents a fragment of frozen time — a way station along the cosmic timestream. The camera records a particular moment of life, capturing it totally, as a fly is caught in amber. Later, that photograph becomes a time machine, taking us back to a precise moment and place, allowing us readmittance to the past. Old memories, lost emotions, are activated.

Case in point: a snapshot on the desk in front of me, dating back to the summer of 1952. Here we all are: me, Fred Brown, Bill Gault and Cleve Cartmill, captured by the lens — Fred, pale, pensive and elfin behind steel-rimmed glasses, with his characteristic wisp of moustache; Gault, solid and tough in an open-neck sport shirt; Cartmill, wry, half-smiling, hands folded over a cane (polio had crippled him early in life); and me, standing to one side, lean, gawky, nervous.

Back then, in that Time of the Snapshot, more than three lost decades ago, we were all living in Southern California. Fred and Bill and Cleve were poker-playing drinking buddies, veteran fellow professionals with a multitude of impressive pulp and slick credits; I was a raw 24-year-old, two years away from my first professional magazine appearance, desperately anxious for a writing career of my own. I looked upon these seasoned pros with awe, respect and envy.

Fred was then in the process of helping launch Gault's book career. *Don't Cry for Me* (1952) was William Campbell Gault's first published novel, issued from Brown's regular publisher, E.P. Dutton, with a generous blurb from Fred on the jacket, praising author and novel.

The gesture was typical. Fred also encouraged me in my early work, openly sharing his knowledge and skills. I found him to be a warm, quiet man with a wacky, pun-loving sense of humor, a sideways thinker who did all of his rough-draft writing inside his head. (His work needed little or no revision from first typescript to printed page.)

He had a special love for music. I'd purchased a new tape recorder that year and I still have a tape of Fred playing his Chinese flute. He had lived in the small town of Taos, New Mexico, before coming to California, and told me that he was "the finest flute player in Taos," adding, with a sly mouse-grin, "that's because no one else in town played a flute."

Fredric William Brown was born, an only child, in Cincinnati, Ohio, in late October of 1906. Fred's mother died of cancer when he was fourteen. His father, a newspaper man, also died when Fred was in his early teens. On his own, in 1922, he obtained a job as office boy with a machine tool company in Cincinnati, Conger & Way, working there into 1924. (He used this background for his autobiographical novel, *The Office,* published in 1959.)

Fred also worked with a traveling carnival during this early period, sharing a tent with the show's mind reader. "I soaked up the atmosphere twenty-four hours a day," he stated in a note for his carny novel, *Madball* (1953), "and it's still in my system." (A carnival theme appeared in many of his tales.)

At twenty, Fred enrolled at Hanover College in Indiana, but spent less than a full year there. He married Helen Brown (no relation) in 1929—and began a 17-year career as a proofreader in Milwaukee in 1930. (I have always found this highly ironic, since Fred's first name was constantly misprinted during his career—as Frederic, Frederick, Fredrick, Fredrik, etc. In fact, years after his death, when I included Fred on the dedication page of my novel, *Logan's World*, a copy editor at Bantam decided that I had not spelled his name correctly, and changed it to "Frederic" on the final galley.)

Proofreading, of course, was never his choice; in his boyhood, Fred had been inspired by Wells, Verne, Burroughs and Jack London, and had formed the dream of becoming a professional writer. Dream became reality in 1938 when he sold his first story to a crime pulp magazine. He began churning out a wide variety of fiction tales for the pulp markets, but could not earn enough at pulp rates to support his wife and two sons. His job as a proofreader helped pay the bills.

Fred attempted to enter the book field in the 1940s, but when his first novel, *The Fabulous Clipjoint*, was rejected by twelve publishers he decided that he had "absolutely no future as a novelist." Then Dutton took a chance and published the book in 1947. By the following year, Fred was in New York accepting the "Edgar" for Best First Novel from the Mystery Writers of America. Dutton's gamble had paid off; they wanted more Fredric Brown mysteries. Fred was forty-one.

"That was the real beginning of my career as a writer," he told me. "With the success of *Clipjoint*, I was able to quit my proofreader's job with the *Milwaukee Journal* and write fulltime."

Fred was divorced the year his book was printed; in 1948 he married Elizabeth Charlier after they'd met at a writers' gathering. They moved to Taos the following year.

"We moved there because of Fred's health," Beth told me. "He suffered from asthma all his life, and needed clear air. We stayed in Taos into the early 1950s."

In New Mexico, Fred took up watercolor painting as a hobby (along with chess, golf and his flute). He wrote and painted at a studio in the historic Governor Bent House in Taos. ("This was the room in which the first American governor of New Mexico was scalped and assassinated in 1848—which provided the perfect climate for my crime fiction.")

By 1952 the Browns had moved to Venice, California (Ray Bradbury's early stomping ground; I'd met Ray there in 1950). Smog was really not a problem in those days, and the ocean breeze kept the air cleared. As co-chairman of the 1952 Westercon (held at the U.S. Grant Hotel in downtown San Diego), I invited Fred to attend as one of the science fiction professionals, along with Bradbury, Cartmill, Kuttner, Neville, Van Vogt, Boucher and others. Fred was "a two-sided writer," equally as well known for his sf work as for his mysteries. He very much enjoyed working in *both* genres.

I recall him at the convention that year—a shy, small, self-effacing man who hated being "in the limelight." But he did favor the company of fellow pros, and appreciated being part of the festivities.

We became fast friends after that convention weekend. We talked a lot about the special problems of plotting, and I recall that he startled me by revealing his offbeat plot method. "I have to do at least one new mystery novel a year for Dutton," he told me. "As each annual deadline nears I become more and more certain I can *never* come up with another decent mystery plot. So I buy a cross-country bus ticket for a round trip to some distant city, ride there and back, thinking *only* about the novel."

He'd always arrive back in California with a full plot worked out in his head. Then he'd sit down and write it.

By 1954 Fred and Beth had left the Los Angeles area to live in Tucson, Arizona. Again, for reasons of health. I was sorry to see him go — but we maintained a warm correspondence and he was very supportive as my own pro career got rolling in the mid 1950s.

We met again in 1961. Fred invited me to have lunch with him in Hollywood. He had come to Los Angeles to write television scripts for the Hitchcock show — and to sell his sf novel, *The Mind Thing,* as a feature film. (The film never jelled, but he did write some teleplays.)

I remember that his hands were shaking. He was fifty-five, thinner than ever, and quite fragile. He told me that he really *liked* Southern California, but could no longer live in the area: "The smog is murder on my bum lungs."

He returned to Tucson.

By the close of 1963, suffering from emphysema, he could no longer write books; his last mystery novel was printed that year.

Fred knew that his career was over. In September of 1971 he confessed in a letter: "Been quite a while since I've done any important creative work."

His condition was terminal. On March 12, 1972, at the age of sixty-five, Fred died of emphysema in Tucson.

What, exactly, did he accomplish in his two dozen active years as a writer? Statistically, we have 28 published novels and several collections encompassing the best of his 270-odd short stories and novelettes (printed in more than 60 magazines, pulp and slick). He completed 22 mystery novels, and these include some of the finest character-suspense studies in the genre. *The Screaming Mimi* has always been one of my personal favorites and his sf novel, *What Mad Universe,* is a true classic. It remains unique: chilling, funny, fast-paced, endlessly inventive. Hallmarks of all his best fiction.

In my Brown collection, I prize a first edition of his boldly-experimental crime tale, *Here Comes a Candle* (". . . to light you to bed. Here comes a chopper to chop off your head!") A stylistic tour de force, the book is written in the form of news clips, straight narrative, radio-play form, as a screenplay, a sportscast, TV script and stage play! And, by God, Fred pulls it off beautifully. A real stunner.

Fred Brown's work reflected the gentle toughness of the man himself, along with his fears, his delight in the bizarre and offbeat, his concern for creating real people in real worlds (and that included his science fictional worlds!); you care about his characters because Fred cared about them.

I have no intention of talking about the stories in this collection; I'm going to allow you to discover the joy in each of them for yourself.

Suffice to say that my old pal, Fred, is alive once again in these pages—with his sly humor, his wickedly-accurate eye for detail, his ability to enchant, shock and surprise.

Believe me, you'll enjoy knowing him.

W.F.N.
May, 1984
Agoura, California

A DATE TO DIE

It was five minutes before five a.m. and the lights in my office at the fourth precinct station were beginning to grow gray with the dawn. To me, that's always the spookiest, least pleasant time of all. Darkness is better, or daylight. And those last five minutes before my relief are always the slowest.

In five minutes Captain Burke would arrive — on the dot, as always — and I could leave. Meanwhile, the hands of the electric clock just crawled.

The ache in my jaw crawled with them. That tooth had started aching three hours ago, and it had kept getting worse ever since. And I wouldn't be able to find a dentist in his office until nine, which was four long hours away. But, come five o'clock, I'd go off duty, and I had a pretty good idea how to deaden the pain a bit while I waited.

Four minutes of five, the phone rang.

"Fourth Precinct," I said, "Sergeant Murray."

"Oh, it's you, Sergeant!" The voice sounded familiar, although I couldn't place it; it was a voice that sounded like an eel feels. "Nice morning, isn't it, Sergeant?"

"Yeah," I growled.

"Of course," said the voice. "Haven't you looked out the window at the pale gray glory that precedes the rising of—"

"Can it," I said. "Who is this?"

"Your friend Sibi Barranya, Sergeant."

I recognized the voice then. It didn't make me any happier to recognize it, because he'd been lying like a rug when he called himself my friend. He definitely wasn't. On the blotter, this mug Barranya is listed as a fortune-teller. He doesn't call himself that; when they play for big dough, the hocus-pocus boys call themselves mystics. That's what Barranya called himself, a mystic. We hadn't been able to pin anything on him, yet.

I said, "So what?"

"I wish to report a murder, Sergeant." His voice sounded slightly bored: you'd have thought I was a waiter and he was ordering lunch. "Your department deals in such matters, I believe."

I knew it was a gag, but I pressed the button that turned on the little yellow light down at the telephone company's switchboard.

I'll explain about that light. A police station gets lots of calls that they have to trace. An excited dame will pick up the phone and say "Help, Police" and bat the receiver back on the hook without bothering to mention who she is or where she lives. Stuff like that. So all calls to any police station in our city go through a special switchboard at the phone station, and the girl who's on that board has special instructions. She never breaks a connection until the receiver has been hung up at the police end of the call, whether the person calling the station hangs up or not. And there's that light that flashes on over her switchboard when we press the button. It's her signal to start tracing a call as quickly as possible.

While I pressed that button, I said, "Nice of you to think of me, Barranya. Who's been murdered?"

"No one, yet, Sergeant. It's murder yet to come. Thought I'd let you in on it."

A DATE TO DIE 13

I grunted. "Picked out who you're going to murder yet, or are you going to shoot at random?"

"Randall," he said, "not random. Charlie Randall, Sergeant. Neighbor of mine; I believe you know him."

Well — on the chance that he was telling the truth and *was* going to commit a murder — I'd as soon have had him pick Randall as anyone. Randall, like Barranya, was a guy we should have put behind bars, except that we had nothing to go on. Randall ran pinball games, which isn't illegal, but we knew (and couldn't prove) some of his methods of squelching opposition. They weren't nice.

Barranya and Randall lived in the same swank apartment building, and it was rumored that the pinball operator was Barranya's chief customer.

All that went through my head, and a lot of other things. Telling it this way, it may sound like I'd been talking over the phone a long time, but actually it had been maybe thirty seconds since I picked up the receiver.

Meanwhile, I had the receiver off the hook of the other phone on my desk — the interoffice one — and was punching the button on its base that would give me the squad car dispatcher at the main station.

I asked Barranya, "Where are you?"

"At Charlie Randall's," he said, "well, here it goes, Sergeant!"

There was the sound of a shot, and then the click of the phone being hung up.

I kept the receiver of that phone to my ear waiting for Central to finish tracing the call, which she'd do right away now that the call had been terminated at that end. Into the other phone I said, "Are you there, Hank?" and the squad car dispatcher said, "Yeah," and I said, "Better put on the radio to — Wait a second."

The other receiver was talking into my other ear now. The gal at Central was saying, "That call came from Woodburn 3480. It's listed as Charles B. Randall, Apart —"

I didn't listen to the rest of it. I knew the apartment number and address. And if it was really Charlie Randall's phone that the call had come over, maybe then Barranya was really telling the truth.

"Hank," I said, "send the nearest car to Randall's apartment, number four at the Deauville Arms. It might be murder."

I clicked the connection to the homicide department, also down at main, and got Captain Holding.

"There might be a murder at number four at the Deauville," I reported. "Charlie Randall. It might be a gag, too. There's a call going out to the nearest squad car; you can wait till they report or start over sooner."

"We'll start over right away," he said. "Nothing to do here anyway."

So that let me out of the game. I stood up and yawned, and by the electric clock on the wall, it was two minutes before five. In two minutes I could leave, and I was going to have three stiff drinks to see if it did my toothache any good. Then I intended going to the Deauville Arms myself. If there was a murder, the homicide boys would want my story about the call. And having something to do would help make the time go faster until nine o'clock when there'd be a dentist available.

If there wasn't a murder, then I wanted a little talk with Sibi Barranya. He might still be there, or up in his own apartment two floors higher. Maybe "talk" isn't the right word. I was going to convince him, with gestures, that I didn't appreciate the gag.

I put on my hat at one minute of five. I looked out the window and saw Captain Burke, who relieves me, getting out of his car across the street.

I opened the door to the waiting room that's between the hall and my office, and took one step into it. Then I stopped — suddenly.

There was a tall, dark, smooth-looking guy sitting there,

A DATE TO DIE 15

looking at one of the picture magazines from the table. He had sharp features and sharp eyes under heavy eyebrows, each of which was fully as large as the small moustache over his thin lips.

There was only one thing wrong with the picture, and that was *who* the guy happened to be. Sibi Barranya — who'd just been talking to me over the telephone a minute before . . . from a point two miles away!

I stood there looking at him, with my mouth open as I figured back. It could have been *two* minutes ago, but no longer. Two minutes, two miles. There's nothing wrong with traveling two miles in two minutes, except that you can't do it when the starting point is the fourth floor of one building and the destination the second floor of another. Besides, the time had been nearer one minute than two.

No, either someone had done a marvelous job of imitating Barranya's voice, or this wasn't him. But this was Barranya, voice and all.

He said, "Sergeant, are you — psychic?"

"Huh?" That was all I could think of at the moment. On top of being where he couldn't be, he had to ask me a completely screwy question.

"The look on your face, Sergeant," he said. "I came here to warn you, and I would swear, from your expression, that you have already received the warning."

"Warn me about what?" I asked.

His face was very solemn. "Your impending death. But you *must* have heard it. Your face, Sergeant. You look like — like you'd had a message from beyond."

Barranya was standing now, facing me, and Captain Burke came in the room from the outer hallway.

"Hello, Murray." He nodded to me. "Something wrong?"

I straightened out my face from whatever shape it had been and said, "Not a thing, Captain, not a thing."

He looked at me curiously, but went on into the inner office.

The more I looked at Barranya, the more I didn't like him, but I decided that whether I liked him or not, he and I had a lot of note-comparing to do. And this wasn't the place to do it.

I said, "The place across the street is open. I like their kind of spirits better than yours. Shall we move there?"

He shook his head. "Thanks, but I'd really better be getting home. Not that I'd mind a drink, but—"

"Somebody's trying to frame a murder rap on you," I told him. "The Deauville Arms is full of cops. Are you still in a hurry?"

It looked as though a kind of film went across his eyes, because they were suddenly quite different from what they had been and yet there had been no movement of eyelid or pupil. It was somehow like the moon going behind a cloud.

He said, "A murder rap means a murder. Whose?"

"Charlie Randall, maybe."

"I'll take that drink," he said. "What do you mean by 'maybe?' "

"Wait a minute and I'll find out." I went back into the inner office, but left the door open so I could keep an eye on Barranya. I said, "Cap, can I use the phone?" and when he nodded, I called the Randall number.

Someone who sounded like a policeman trying to sound like a butler said, "Randall residence."

"This is Bill Murray. Who's talking?"

"Oh," said the voice, not sounding like a butler any longer. "This is Kane. We just busted in. I was going to the phone to call main when it rang and I thought I'd try to see who was—"

"What'd you find?"

"There's a stiff here, all right. I guess it's Randall; I never saw him, but I've seen his pictures in the paper and it looks like him."

"Okay," I said. "The homicide squad's already on the way over. Just hold things down till they get there. I'm coming around too, but I got something to do first. Say—how was he killed?"

A DATE TO DIE 17

"Bullet in the forehead. Looks like about a thirty-eight hole. He's sitting right there; I'm looking at him now. Harry's going over the apartment. I was just going to the phone to call—"

"Yeah," I interrupted. "Is he tied up?"

"Tied up, yes. He's in pajamas, and there's a bruise on his forehead, but he isn't gagged. Looks like he was slugged in bed and somebody moved him to the chair and tied him to it, and then took a pop at him with the gun from about where I'm standing now."

"At the phone?"

"Sure, at the phone. Where else would I be standing?"

"Well," I said, "I'll be around later. Tell Cap Holding when he gets there."

"Know who done it, Sarge?"

"It's a secret," I said, and hung up.

I went back to the inner office. Barranya was standing by the door. I knew he'd heard the conversation so I didn't need to tell him he could erase the 'maybe' about Charlie Randall's being dead.

We went across the street to Joe's, which is open twenty-four hours a day. It was five minutes after five when we got there, and I noticed that it took us a few seconds over two minutes just to get from my office to Joe's, which is half a block.

We took a booth at the back. Barranya took a highball, but I wanted mine straight and double. My tooth was thumping like hell.

I said, "Listen, Barranya, first let's take this warning business. About me, I mean. What kind of a hook-up did it come over?"

"A voice," he said. "I've heard voices many times, but this was louder and clearer than usual. It said, 'Sergeant Murray will be killed today.'"

"Did it say anything else?"

"No, just that. Over and over. Five or six times."

"And where were you when you heard this voice?"

"In my car, Sergeant, driving—let's see—along Clayton Boulevard. About half an hour ago."

"Who was with you?"

"No one, Sergeant. It was a spirit voice. When one is psychic, one hears them often. Sometimes meaningless things, and sometimes messages for oneself or people one knows."

I stared at him, wondering whether he really expected me to swallow that. But he had a poker face.

I took a fresh tack. "So, out of the kindness of your heart you came around to warn me. Knowing that for a year now I've been trying to get something on you so I could put you—"

His upraised hand stopped me. "That is something else again, Sergeant. I don't particularly like you personally, but a psychic has obligations which transcend the mundane. If it was not intended that I pass that warning on to you, I should not have received it."

"Where had you been, before this happened?"

"I went with a party of people to the Anders Farm."

The Anders Farm isn't a farm at all; it's a roadhouse and it's about fifteen miles out of town. Coming on from there, you take Highway 15, which turns into Clayton Boulevard in town.

"I left the others there around four o'clock," Barranya said. "We'd been there since midnight and I was getting bored, and—well, feeling queer—as often happens when I am on the verge of a communication from the astral—"

"Wait," I said, "were you there with someone? A woman?"

"No, Sergeant. It was a mixed party, but there were three couples and two stags and I was one of the stags. I drove slowly coming in, because I'd been drinking and because of that feeling of expectancy. I was on Clayton, out around Fiftieth, when I heard the voice. It said, 'Sergeant Murray will be killed to—' "

"Yeah, yeah," I interrupted. For some reason, it made my tooth

A DATE TO DIE   19

ache worse when he said that. I looked at him a minute trying to figure out how much truth he was telling me. I couldn't swallow that spirit message stuff.

But the rest of it? It would be easy to get and check the names of the people he'd been with. But that was routine, up to whoever was handling the case. . . .

Say Barranya left the Anders Farm near four o'clock. He came to my office at five, or a few minutes before. That gave him an hour. Not too long a time if he'd driven as slowly as he said. But it was possible.

I said, "Now about Charlie Randall. What were your relations with him?"

"Very pleasant, Sergeant. I advised him in a business way."

I studied him. "Meaning when he had to bump off a competitor you'd cast a horoscope to see if the stars were favorable?"

That veil business was over his eyes again, and I knew he didn't like the way I'd put that. It was probably a close guess. We knew that Randall, like most crooks, was superstitious and that he was Sibi Barranya's best hocus-pocus sucker.

Barranya said, "Mr. Randall conducted a legitimate business, Sergeant. My advice concerned purely legal transactions."

"No doubt," I said. "Since it would be hard to prove otherwise now, we'll let it ride. But look—you're probably pretty familiar with Randall's business. Who would benefit by his death?"

Barranya thought a moment before he answered. "His wife, of course. That is, I presume she'll inherit his money; he never consulted me about a will. And there is Pete Burd; but you know about that."

I knew about Pete Burd, all right. He was the only rival Randall had had, and not too much competition at that. He put his machines in the smaller places that Randall didn't want, and that was maybe why Randall hadn't done to him what he'd done to more enterprising competitors. But now that Randall was out of the way, it would mean room for expansion for Burd.

I let that cook for the moment. "Know where Charlie's wife is?"

"Yes. Out of town. That is, unless she has returned unexpectedly and I haven't heard."

I snorted lightly. "Don't your spirits tell you things? . . . Let's get back to the warning about me. Did the what's-it suggest any reason why I might be killed?"

"No," he told me, "and I can see you're incredulous about that, Sergeant. Frankly, I don't care whether you take it seriously or not. I had a message and it was my duty to relay it. Any more questions? If not, I'd like to get on home."

I stood up. "We're both going to the same building. Come on."

"Fine!" Barranya said. "Want to go in my car? I presume there'll be plenty of squad cars rallying around over there to give you a lift back."

Well, there would be; and these days a chance to save rubber is a chance to save rubber. So I got into his car. And when I saw how smoothly it ran I wondered — as all cops wonder once in a while, but not too seriously — whether I'd picked the right side of the law. It was a sweet chariot, that convertible of his.

"Can you get short-wave broadcasts?" I asked, assuming that a boat like his would have a radio, and ready not to be surprised if it turned out to be a radio-phono combination. I was curious to see if anything new was going out to the squad cars.

"Out of order," he said. "Worked early this evening, but I tried it after I left the Anders Farm and it wouldn't work."

We drove a few blocks without either of us saying anything, and it was then that I heard the voice:

"Sibi Barranya killed Randall. He wanted Randall's wife."

I blinked and looked around at Barranya. He wasn't talking, unless he was a good ventriloquist. Not that it would have surprised me if he was, because these fake mystics dabble in all forms of trickery.

A DATE TO DIE 21

But Barranya looked scared as hell. The car swerved a little, but righted itself as he swung the wheel back. We slowed up and he said, "Did you hear—"

"Shut up," I barked. As soon as I'd seen his lips weren't moving, I looked around the rest of the car. Maybe it was the comparative quiet because we were slowing down, but I recognized and placed a faint sound I'd been hearing ever since we'd started; a sound I'd wondered about in a car that ran as sweet and smooth as that one did.

It was a faint crackling, like static on a radio, and it seemed to come from the loud-speaker that was up where the windshield met the car top, on Barranya's side.

"Cut in to the curb and stop a minute," I said.

As we coasted in, he said, "Sergeant, there are good spirits and evil ones. The evil ones lie, and you mustn't—"

"Shut up," I said. "There are good radios and bad radios, too. Where's a screwdriver?"

He opened the glove compartment and found one. "Do you mean you think—"

I said, "I'm sure as hell going to see. When it comes to spooks, Barranya, I don't think anything. I look for where they come from. That radio's on!"

I got it out from behind the instrument panel with the screwdriver. The faint crackling noise stopped when I disconnected the battery wire.

The set showed what I had a hunch I'd find. It had been tampered with, all right. There was a wire shorted across both the short-wave band switch and the turn-on switch, so that it was permanently on, and permanently adjusted to the short-wave band. The condenser shaft had been loosened so the rotor plates didn't turn with the shaft. In other words, it was permanently set to receive anything broadcast on a certain short wavelength.

Barranya was peering curiously at it. "Could someone with an amateur broadcasting set have? . . ."

"They could," I told him, "and did. How's your battery?"

"How's — Oh, I see what you mean." Without putting the car in gear he stepped on the starter and the engine turned over merrily. The battery wasn't run down.

"This thing's been on," I said, "since it was monkeyed with. If your battery's still got that much oomph, it means it was done recently. If your radio worked early this evening, this was done since then. Maybe while you were at the roadhouse."

"Then that other message, the one that warned about you—"

"Yeah," I said, "my apologies—maybe. I thought you were talking a lot of hot air."

Unless he was honestly bewildered, he was putting on a marvelous act. He said, "But I have heard such voices elsewhere."

I smiled. "Maybe your radio here was in tune with the infinite and it was a spirit, once removed. I got my doubts. Let's get going. I want to show this little gadget to the boys."

He slid the car into gear and away from the curb. He asked thoughtfully, "Is there any way they could trace from that set where the messages came from?"

"Nope," I told him. "But they can tell exactly what wavelength it was set for. That might help, but the F.C.C. has suspended all amateur licenses since the war started. It would have to be an illegal set."

"Aren't illegal broadcasts tracked down?"

"Yeah. There are regular listening posts, with directional equipment. But if a set broadcast only a couple of sentences like that, they'd probably be overlooked. So that's no help."

We were slowing down already for the apartment building when I remembered. "How's about what your radio ghost friend said just now? Are you chummy with Randall's wife?"

He took time to word his answer. I could have counted to ten before he said, "You'd find out anyway, I suppose. Yes, I like her a lot and she likes me. Her husband. . . ."

A DATE TO DIE 23

"Didn't understand her?" I prompted.

He glared at me, and started to say something that would probably have led to trouble if I'd let him finish.

"Hold it, pal," I cut in. "Here's the big thing to think about. Whoever put on that broadcast just now knew about you and Mrs. Randall. How many people know that. Pete Burd, maybe?"

He calmed down. "I don't know. Anyone might have guessed, I suppose. Uh—Charlie Randall didn't mind, so we weren't too secretive about being seen."

"Randall *knew* you were making love to his wife!"

"I think so. He wouldn't have cared, if he had known. You know that little blonde who used to sell cigarettes at the Green Dragon?"

"I think I know which one you mean," I told him. "The one with the nice—"

"That one," he said. "She doesn't work there any more."

The car stopped in front of the Deauville Arms, and I got out, carrying the gimmicked radio. I waited until Barranya came around the car to join me.

When we got into the elevator I said, "We're going to Randall's flat first, both of us. You'll have to bear up a while yet before you go to sleep."

"Why can't I go on up, while you—"

"Nix," I said. "I'm going to report to Holding, and you're not going in that flat before I go with you. Listen, Barranya, the only thing I don't like about your alibi is that it's too damn good. Maybe you got something upstairs I'd like to see before you dismantle it. Such like a phonograph with your—"

I broke off, because as soon as I mentioned it I knew it wasn't a phonograph record that had made that call. Because I'd done part of the talking, and he'd answered what I said. I remembered that lousy gag about not shooting at random but at Randall.

But I took Barranya with me just the same. Holding would want to see him.

The Randall flat was full of photographers and fingerprint men. I parked Barranya in the hallway, and told the man on duty at the door to keep an eye on him. I went in to give Holding my report and the radio set.

The coroner was working on the body; they'd moved it into the bedroom after taking photos. Captain Holding showed me the position of the chair and the ropes; everything checked with what I'd heard over the telephone.

Holding said, "Maybe Barranya could have called you from the phone booth in the hall at your precinct station, and then gone on into the waiting room while—"

"No, dammit," I said. "I traced the call. It came from here. It must be some kind of a frame, but it's the goofiest thing I ever heard of. If anybody wanted to frame Barranya, why'd they give him that message about me that sent him to my office only two minutes after the murder?"

Holding shrugged. "Do you know anybody connected with the case who's a good voice imitator?"

"Not unless it's Barranya, and he wouldn't imitate his own voice. Nuts! I'm going in circles, and this toothache is driving me batty. Say, how's Mrs. Randall doing on alibis?"

"Excellent. We called the hotel in Miami she was supposed to be at. She's there all right. I talked to her myself."

"Just now?"

"What do you mean, just now? Think we could have notified her yesterday, Sergeant?"

I shook my head. "Don't mind me, Cap. My mind just isn't working any more. But one thing. I take it you're going to send men up to search Barranya's place. Maybe while he's here and you're talking to him? Well, I'd like to go up with them."

"You should go home, Bill. This is our job, now that you've reported," Holding pointed out.

"Got to stay awake till I can see a dentist at nine. Having

something to do will keep my mind off this damn toothache. Anyway, this is my big day, Cap. If Barranya's spirit controls are in working order, I'm due to be bumped off."

"I'll question Barranya now. I'll hold him a while, and give you plenty of time, though."

"Swell. I'm even going to take the kitchen sink apart up there. Say, know who lives above and below this flat — on the third and fifth?"

"Third's vacant. Guy named Shultz has the fifth, in between here and Barranya."

"What's he do?" I asked.

"Manufacturer. Pinball games and carnival novelties." Holding saw the sudden look of interest I gave him, and went on. "Yes, he did a little business with Randall. But he's clear on this. He's out of town, he and his wife. We've checked and it's on the up and up."

"How about Burd?"

"Murphy's on the way over there now. I'm going to have that cigarette girl angle looked into, too. We can trace her easy enough if Randall set her up somewhere. Might be an angle there."

"More curves than angles," I said. "Sure you don't want *me* to —"

"I do not. Send in Barranya, and take Clem and Harry up to his flat."

Clem and Harry and I spent two hours searching, but there wasn't anything in Barranya's flat worthy of interest except a bottle of Scotch in the cupboard. The homicide boys didn't touch it because they were on duty, but I wasn't.

When they left, I sat down at the table in the living room to wait. Holding kept Barranya down there another half hour. He looked mad when he came in. By that time my tooth had stopped jumping up and down and settled into a slow steady ache that wasn't quite so bad.

I waved my hand toward the Scotch on the table, and the extra glass I'd put there. "Have a drink."

"Thanks, Sergeant, I shall. After that, if you don't mind, I'd like to turn in."

"Don't mind me," I told him. "Go right ahead and turn in. It's your flat."

"But—" He looked puzzled.

"Don't mind me, I'm just sitting here thinking."

He poured himself a drink from the bottle and refilled my glass. He said, "And how long do you expect to sit there and think?"

"Until I've figured out how you killed Charlie Randall."

He smiled, and sat down on a corner of the table. He said, "What makes you think I killed Randall?"

"The fact that you *couldn't* have," I told him, very earnestly. "It's all too damn pat, Barranya. It's like a stage illusion. It's a show. It doesn't ring true. It's just the kind of murder and kind of alibi that an illusionist would arrange. The kind of thing that wouldn't occur to an ordinary guy."

"You're logical, Sergeant, up to a point."

"And I'm going to get past that point. Go on to bed if you're tired."

He chuckled and stared down into the amber liquid in his glass. "Is that all that makes you think I did it?"

"Not quite," I said. "We found something very suspicious in this flat. That's what makes me sure."

He looked up quickly.

"We found *nothing*, Barranya. Absolutely nothing of interest."

His smile came back; mockingly, I thought. "And you find that suspicious?"

"Absolutely. I have a strong hunch that before you left here this evening you took away and hid any papers, any notations, you wouldn't have wanted the police to find. And the gimmicks connected with the seances you hold here."

"They aren't seances. I've explained—"

A DATE TO DIE 27

"It's just unlikely," I went on without paying any attention to his interruption, "for us not to have found *something* you wouldn't want found. Not even letters tied in blue ribbon. Not a scrap of a notation about one of your customers."

"Clients."

"Clients, then. Nothing at all. I just don't believe it, Barranya. And if you knew this apartment would be searched, then you knew Randall was going to be killed. That means you killed him, somehow."

"Brilliant, Sergeant. Have your deductions gone any farther?"

"Yes. You knew when he was going to be killed — or when it would appear that he was killed. Probably it was twenty minutes before I got that phone call. Time for you to get from his flat to my office."

"And you think I framed myself by accusing —"

"Why not? That radio was a swell trick. It wasn't the radio at all, Barranya. I've thought that out. It *was* ventriloquism. My first guess was right, only I found that radio going and naturally thought that the voice came from it. You fixed the radio yourself, and any spiritualist knows ventriloquism — the safest and easiest way of getting spirit voices in a seance. The trick has whiskers on it."

He said, "Interesting, Sergeant — if you can prove that I do know ventrilo —"

"I can't, but I'm not interested. All I have to prove is that you killed Randall. As long as I know you *could* have pulled that stunt in the car, I can forget it. How's about another drink? And incidentally, *what* you said was clever as hell. You knew we'd find out about you and Mrs. Randall, and if you accused yourself of having that motive, it would spike our guns. You expect to marry her, don't you, and get Randall's money?"

He filled my glass, but not his own. He stood up, yawning. "Hope you'll excuse me, Sergeant. I *am* tired."

"Go right to bed," I said. "Got an alarm clock, or shall I wake you any special time?"

"Never mind." He sauntered to the door of the bedroom and then turned. "I'll appreciate your leaving one drink in the bottle."

"I'll buy you a new bottle," I assured him. "Barranya, you know anything about relays?"

"Relays? I'm not sure I know what you mean."

"I'm not, either. Probably that's the wrong name for it. But it's the first thing I looked for when I came up here. I didn't find it."

"And where would you have looked for one?"

"I thought of the bell box of your telephone. Look, while you were playing Randall for a sucker on the celestial advice racket, didn't you have his phone wire tapped?"

"No, Sergeant. But how would a tapped wire—"

"Here's the idea. Holding gave it to me, in a way. He said you might have phoned from the booth at the station, right out in the hall. Except that the call came from here, that would have made sense. So I got to thinking."

"So?"

"This could have happened. You came here, driving fast from the roadhouse, killed Randall, and switched in the gimmick. You'd have everything ready, so you could do it in a minute. There'd already be the tap on Randall's wire. The gimmick is a little electromagnet in your phone's bell box.

"You drive to the station and call *your own* phone. The circuit is shorted through the electromagnet, so instead of ringing the bell, the magnet throws the double switch—just as though the receiver had been lifted from Randall's phone. You're on Randall's wire and when the light goes on down at the phone company switchboard, it's over his number. That switch also opens his circuit, of course. When Central says 'Number, please?' you give my number, and—well, that's all it would take. You knew, of course, that snapping a rubber band across the diaphram of the transmitter makes a sound like a shot.

A DATE TO DIE 29

"And when you hung up, both circuits would be broken, and things just like they were. The call would trace back to Randall's phone, but his receiver was never off the hook!"

Barranya's eyes had widened while I was talking. He said, "Sergeant, I never thought it of you. That's positively brilliant. But you didn't find such an electromagnet?"

"No," I admitted. "But it was a good idea."

He yawned again. "You underestimate yourself. It was excellent. Pardon me."

"I will," I said, "but how about the governor?"

He chuckled and closed the bedroom door. I poured myself another drink, but I didn't touch it. The last three drinks hadn't had any further effect on the toothache, so I figured I might as well stay sober and bear it.

I listened until I heard him get into bed. Then I gave it another ten minutes by my watch.

I went out the door and closed it, being neither quiet nor noisy about my movements, got into the elevator and—in case the sound of the elevator would be audible—I rode it all the way down to the first floor and walked back up to five. One of my set of keys worked easily on the door of the absent Mr. Shultz.

I crossed over to the telephone and bent down to examine the box. There wasn't any dust on top of it, and there *was* a thin layer of dust on most other things in the room.

I didn't touch it. I was sure enough now that the electromagnet would be there, and I didn't want to lessen its value as evidence by taking off the cover until there were other witnesses. Anyway, there was an easier way to check my hunch.

I picked up the receiver and when a feminine voice said, "Number, please?" I asked, "What phone am I calling from?"

"Pardon?"

I said, "I'm alone at a friend's house. I want to tell someone to call me back here, and I can't read the number without my glasses."

She said, "Oh, I see. You're calling from Woodburn 3840."

Randall's number. That cracked the case, of course. Barranya had worked it just as I'd told him upstairs, except that, knowing his own flat would be searched, he'd put the tab on Shultz' phone and called up there.

"Fine," I said, "Now give me —"

That was when something jabbed into my back and Barranya said, "Tell her never mind." His tone of voice meant business.

"Never mind," I told the operator. "I'll put in the call later."

As I put down the phone, Barranya's hand reached over my shoulder and slid my police positive out of its shoulder holster. He stepped back, and I turned around.

He'd really undressed for bed; he wore a lounging robe over pajamas and had slippers on his feet. That's why I hadn't heard him come through the flat. I'd known he'd be down sometime today to remove the evidence, but I'd expected him to wait longer, and I hadn't thought of the back door. Maybe I'd drunk more Scotch than I thought I had, to overlook a bet like that.

His face was expressionless; there was just a touch of mockery in his voice. "Remember that message I brought you from the spirit world a few hours ago, Sergeant? Maybe it wasn't as wrong as you thought."

"You can't get away with it," I said. "Killing me, I mean. If you do, you'll have to lam, and they'll catch you. The homicide boys know I stayed with you. If they find me dead —"

"Shut up, Sergeant," he said, "I'm trying to think how —"

I didn't dare give him time to think. The guy was too clever. He might think of some way he could kill me without it being pinned on him.

I said, "A good lawyer can get you a sentence for shooting a rat like Randall. But you know what happens when you kill a cop in this state."

I could see there was indecision in his face, in his voice when he said, "Keep back, or —"

A DATE TO DIE

I took another step toward him and kept on talking. I said, "There are still men in Randall's flat, right under us. They'll hear that gun. You won't have time to muffle it, like when you shot Randall."

I kept walking, slowly. I knew if I moved suddenly, he'd shoot. My hands were going down slowly, too. I said, "Give me that gun, Barranya. Figure out what a rope around your neck feels like before you pull that trigger, and don't pull it."

I was reaching out, palm upward for him to hand the gun to me, but he backed away. He said, "Stop, damn you," and the urbanity and mockery were gone from his voice. He was scared.

I kept walking forward. I said, "I saw a cop-killer once after they finished questioning him, Barranya. They did such a job that he didn't mind hanging, much, after that. And don't forget the boys below us will hear a shot. You won't have time to pull those wires up through the wall before they get up here."

And then he was back against the wall, and I must have pressed him too hard, because I saw from his eyes that he was going to shoot. But my hand was only inches from the gun now, and I took the last short step in a lunge and slapped the gun just as it went off. I felt the burn of powder on my palm and wrist, but I wasn't hit. The gun hit the wall and ricocheted under the sofa.

The burn on my hand made me jerk back, involuntarily, off balance, and he jumped in with a wallop that caught me on the jaw that knocked me further off balance.

I took half a dozen punches, and they hurt, before I could get set to throw one back effectively. I took half a dozen more before I got in my Sunday punch and Barranya folded up on the carpet.

I staggered across the room to the phone. My nose felt lopsided and one of my eyes was hard to see out of. There was blood in my mouth and I spat it out. A tooth came with it.

I got Holding on the phone, and told him. I said, "I guess there's no one downstairs at the moment or they'd sure as hell be up here by now."

He said, "Swell work, Sarge. We'll be right over; sit on the guy till we get there. How's your toothache coming?"

"Huh?" I said, and then it dawned on me that my whole face and head ached, except for my tooth. I felt to see which one had been knocked out in the fight, and it was!

After I'd hung up, I found Shultz, too, was a good ghost; his whiskey was poorly hidden. My knees felt wobbly and I figured I'd earned this one. I had another, and then heard voices and footsteps out in the hall, and knew the homicide boys were back.

I walked over to the sofa where Barranya lay, to see if he was conscious again. He wasn't, but bending over made my head swim and suddenly my knees just weren't there any more. I don't know whether it was the whiskey, or the fight I'd been through, or the relief that I didn't have to go to the dentist.

But I'll never live down the fact that they came in a second later—and found me sleeping peacefully on top of the murderer.

MAD DOG!

I got it the minute I saw that distorted face peering around the corner of the turn in the hallway. I wasn't looking toward the hallway, of course, but toward MacCready. Back of Mac's desk was a mirror and it was in the mirror that I saw it.

For just a minute I thought I had 'em, then I remembered Mac's screwy ideas on mental therapeutics, and I grinned. I kept the grin to myself, though. Here's where I have some fun with good old Mac, I thought to myself. Let him pull his gag and pretend to play along.

So I kept on with what I was saying. "Mac, old horse," I told him, "can't you get it out of your head that this isn't a professional call? Quit psychoanalyzing me, dammit, or I'll leave you flat and hike right back to Provincetown over these bloody rollercoaster anthills you call dunes, and get myself drunk."

He snorted, a well-bred Scotch snort. "You'd fall flat on your face before you got halfway. Bryce, how you ever made it out here's got me beat. And how you ever write plays that get on Broadway, when you keep yourself so full of whiskey that—" He shook his head in bewilderment.

"Ever see any of my plays, Mac? Maybe you'd get the connection. But—"

I caught sight of that face again in the mirror, and I calculated the angle and decided that Mac couldn't see it from where he sat. The guy in the hall had come around the corner now, and was pussy-footing up to the door. He was smiling, if you could call it a smile; one corner of his mouth went up and the other down so his mouth looked like an unhealed diagonal wound across the bottom of his face. His eyes were so narrowed you couldn't see the whites. I thought crazily that if the British had done that at Bunker Hill they wouldn't have got fired on at all.

All in all it wasn't a nice expression. I shuddered a bit, involuntarily. Whoever was stooging for Mac on this gag of his ought to be on the stage. He could do Dracula without makeup, unless he already had the makeup on, and if he did, it was a wow.

Mac was talking again, it dawned on me. "If this wasn't my vacation—" he was saying. "Listen, Bryce, even if it is, I'll take you on. It'd take me three months to get you wrung out so you'd stay that way, but I'll do it if you say the word. You're darned far on the road to being an alcoholic. At the rate you're going, pal. . . ."

I grinned at him. "You underestimate me, old horse. I'm a lush of the first water, right now. I like it. But listen, Mac, there is something that worries me. I'm three months overdue on starting my next play, and I haven't a ghost of an idea. I thought a summer in Provincetown would fix me up. Cape Cod and all that and the picturesque fishing smacks and all that sort of tripe. But—well, I'm worried stiff."

I was, too. There's nothing worse than not having an idea when you need an idea. That's the trouble with being a playwright. If you need a house or a horse or a multiple-head drill or a set of golf clubs, you go out and buy it, but if you need an idea and need it bad, you sit and stew and maybe it comes and maybe it doesn't. If it doesn't, you go slowly nuts.

You get to the stage where you remember that an old friend

MAD DOG! 35

of yours is a psychiatrist and has his summer home on the other side of the cape, with the waves of the Atlantic rolling into his front yard, and you hike across the dunes to see him to find out what's wrong that you haven't got an idea.

He said, "How to help you there, Bryce, I'm not sure. But this should be good country for you. Eugene O'Neill got his start here, and Millay, and others. Harry Kemp has a place only a few miles from here, and . . ."

That was when the guy in the hallway reached around the door jamb and switched off the light. Mac's head—I could still see dimly because it was only eight-thirty and not completely dark out yet what with daylight savings time and a bright moon—jerked around toward the doorway and I saw his eyes widen. He reached quick for a drawer of his desk and then slowly started to raise his hands up over his head instead. He was going to take it big, I could see that.

I turned my head slowly toward the doorway. The man had stepped fully into the room now, and although his face was in the shadow now, I could see how big and powerful he was. He wore an overcoat three sizes too large for him, and he held something in his hand that looked like a cross between a pistol and a shotgun. It must be, I decided, a scattergun—one of those things cautious householders keep on hand for burglars. It's useless at any range to speak of, but up to twenty feet it can't miss a man, and it can't miss doing unpleasant things to him. It shoots a small gauge shotgun shell.

Of course, this one wouldn't be loaded. Maybe my pal Colin MacCready didn't know I'd read his most recent book, but I had. In it, he told his ideas about what he called "shock treatment." Alcoholism was one of the things it was supposed to help. I won't go into details, but the basic idea is to scare the pants off the patient.

He'd described several ways of doing it; apparently the treatment was varied to suit the individual case. I personally thought the idea was screwy when I read about it, but then I'm not a psychiatrist, thank heaven. Anyhow, it sounded interesting, and for a moment I wished that that book hadn't tipped me off in advance so I could tell how I'd feel if things really were what they were maybe going to be.

The guy with the gun was talking now, to Mac. He said, "Come out from behind that desk, Doc. You and this other mug stand close together. Who is he?"

What faint light came in the window fell on Mac's face when he stood up, and he was doing it well. He didn't look frightened, but he looked deadly serious, and a little pale. He kept his hands up level with his shoulders. He started to edge around the desk toward my chair. Then his face got into the shadow again.

He said, "This is just a friend of mine, Herman. Now—when did you escape?"

I stood up and bowed ceremoniously. If I'd been sober, by that time I'd have been suspecting my diagnosis of the situation. There was something just a little phony about it to be wrong. It was too slow an approach, it lacked the zip and tempo, the suddenness of shock described in that book. But I wasn't sober, quite.

Anyhow, I bowed low and said, "Dr. Livingstone, I presume," or something equally idiotic, and started across the room toward the guy Mac had just addressed as Herman. The gun jerked up in my direction.

I heard Mac call out sharply, "Don't shoot! I'll—" and I didn't hear the rest of it for something that must have been Mac's fist clouted me on the side of the jaw. Mac is no lightweight and that wallop had, I guessed, his whole weight behind it. I went down, groggy, but not completely out.

Something—it must have been common sense—told me to stay there. I heard Mac say, "Whew!" and this guy Herman say

MAD DOG! 37

coldly, "Another funny move like that from either of you—"

"Another funny move won't happen, Herman," said Mac, soothingly. "My friend is a little drunk, that's all. Quite a little. What can I do for you?"

"First, you will tie up your friend so I'll not have to watch him. Who else is in the house?"

I heard Mac say, "No one, Herman. I have one servant but he has the day off. Drove in to Wellfleet."

He was telling the truth, I knew. That proved nothing one way or the other, of course. Mac said, "There's rope in the kitchen, Herman. Shall I—"

"Take off his necktie and yours, Doc. You tie his ankles with one and his wrists, behind him, with the other. Tight."

Mac came over and untied my cravat. He pretended to have trouble unknotting it, and bent down close and whispered. "Careful, Bryce. Homicidal maniac. Escaped. I had to sock you or—"

He didn't have to finish that "or—" if the rest of it was true. At an order from the man with the scattergun, he stepped back. At another order, he opened a drawer in his desk in which he kept a gun and then stepped back flat against the wall while the maniac pocketed the gun.

Then he said, "Sit down, Doc." He kept the scattergun in his hand ready for action.

I'd rolled over, cautiously, so I could keep an eye on what went on. Mac had tied my wrists and ankles, and had done a good job of it, probably thinking he'd be checked up on it. I saw Mac cross cautiously to the desk and sit down.

He said, "What are you going to do, Herman?"

Sitting at the desk, Mac was in what little light came in from the windows. The other man was now nothing but a huge dark shadow standing there. He didn't say anything for a moment, and in the silence you could hear the waves lapping on the shore outside and the far squeaky cry of a circling gull.

He said, "I'm going back to finish. To kill the rest of them. Do you think I'm crazy?" He laughed a little, as though he had said something very funny.

"Your father and your brother both?" Mac's voice was quiet. "Why? Your sister—well, I thought you killed her, Herman, because there was always enmity between you. But Kurt—what have you got against Kurt? Why should you want to kill your brother?"

The madman chuckled. His voice started out soft, almost a whisper in the darkness, and got louder. "The *ears,* Doc. Like the rest of them. Dad, too. I never told anybody about that, but I didn't really hate Lila, except for them. Those damned ears—they—"

Unless it was magnificent acting, he was starkly mad. His voice had risen in pitch and volume until he was shouting meaningless obscenities. I heard Mac's voice cut in quietly, calmly.

"Herman—"

"You can't stop me, Doc. I—I just stopped here to show you that I'm *not* crazy, like you said I was at the hearing. See? Why don't I kill you? This friend of yours? Because I don't *have* to. I'll shoot you in a minute if you try to stop me, both of you, but if what you said about me was true, why don't I do it now?"

He went on arguing, calmer now, sometimes talking almost sensibly, sometimes with the perverted logic of paranoia. Mac egged him on, tried to reason with him from his own premises, tried to convince him without contradicting flatly any of the madman's statements.

I started quietly to work on the knots in the cravat that held my wrists behind me. I knew Mac was stalling, trying to hold the fellow as long as he could. He wasn't stalling for help from me. I knew that from the way he'd tied those blamed knots so tightly. He figured me as a liability rather than an asset after that fool stunt I'd pulled, and I couldn't blame him for that. But I went to work on those knots just the same.

MAD DOG!

"You won't believe me, Doc," I heard Herman say. "All right, so you won't. But don't think I don't know why you're stalling. You think they're after me, and will trail me here." He laughed again.

"How did you get away, Herman?"

"They aren't after me, Doc. Not here, I mean. They've got a swamp surrounded back ten miles from the sanitarium, and I'm supposed to be in it, armed, and they're taking their time. I've got till morning. I've got lots of time. It's just getting dark now."

"Herman, you won't get away with it. They'll catch you and —"

"And what? Listen, I'm crazy; you said so and you swore to it, and other doctors, too. If they do catch me, what can they do but put me back, see? I'm going to tie you up now, Doc, so you won't go running for help. Stand up and turn around."

"I'm anxious to talk to you more about your father and about Kurt. Herman, you mustn't —"

"I've talked enough, Doc. Get up. And before I tie you, I'm going to hit you on the head hard enough to knock you out, because I don't want any trouble. But I won't hit hard enough to kill you."

Mac's voice again, persuasively; the madman's, sharper. He took a step nearer the desk, and that put him within a yard of where I lay. Those knots hadn't budged a millimeter. But, standing where the guy was, and with Mac on hand to finish what I could start, I saw a chance.

If I swiveled around and doubled up my legs and lashed them out right at the back of his knees, he'd go down like a ton of bricks. And Mac is no mean scrapper; he should have been able to take over from there.

Maybe if I'd been cold sober, I wouldn't have been ready to take a chance like that. But I wasn't. And I wasn't entirely convinced that there wasn't something phony about the set-up. It seemed just a bit theatrical to be true, like a second act that needs patching.

Anyway, I braced my wrists and heels against the floor and swiveled myself around, and I made enough noise in doing it to make the guy with the scattergun take a quick look around behind him to see what was going on. And that was the end of my little scheme.

I suppose I was lucky he didn't pot me with the gun, but my luck didn't seem so hot at the moment, for he pulled back his foot and lashed out a kick at my head that would have killed me if it had landed squarely.

And it missed landing squarely by a narrow margin. I jerked under it and the toe of his shoe passed safely over, the heel catching my mouth a glancing but painful blow. There was a taste of blood in my mouth — and the realization that I'd come within less than an inch of losing my front teeth. Then and there I abandoned any doubt I'd had about whether that gun was loaded and whether the man holding it was playing for keeps.

I could hear, but not see, Mac starting across the desk, trying to close in during the diversion I'd caused. But he didn't have time. The maniac swung back, raised the barrel of that scattergun and brought it down on Mac's head with a sickening thump. Mac's momentum carried him on across the desk and he fell unconscious, on the floor near me.

There didn't seem to be anything to say, so I didn't say it, and the silence was so thick you could spread it with a knife. The guy who had just slugged Mac grunted once, then he went out toward the kitchen and came back with some heavy twine, a ball of it. He kept an eye on me while he tied up Mac.

Then he said, "You going to lie still while I put some of this on you, or —" He hefted the gun significantly, a shadowy bludgeon in the gathering darkness.

"I'll lie still," I told him. "Is — Mac — all right?"

He came over and began to supplement the two neckties that held my wrists and ankles with wrappings of the twine. "Sure," he said, "he's breathing. I should have killed him and you, too, but—"

He was finishing my ankles now.

I'd been thinking. Maybe I was getting sober or maybe I was just beginning to feel the effect of what I'd drunk; I don't know. Anyway, along with the taste of blood in my mouth was a taste of something strictly phony. I knew now, of course, that this wasn't any idea of Mac's, but it was still a bad second act.

Yes, that was it—call it a playwright's instinct, but this was a *second* act; there'd been a first one that I didn't know about. I'd walked in during the intermission.

"Listen," I said, "why did you come here at all, *really?*"

The moment the words were out, I knew I shouldn't have said it. He'd just stood up, and the gun was still in his pocket where he'd stuck it to tie me up. Slowly he took it out again, and, like he was thinking hard while he was doing it, he swung the muzzle around until it pointed at my head.

At times like that, you think crazy things. The first thought that popped into my head, while that gun was swinging around was—"This tears it. It's going to be a *hell* of a second act curtain, with the hero getting killed!" Sure, I thought of myself as the hero. I don't know why; but who doesn't?

That screwy notion, though, took just about as long to flash through my head as it took the gun to move an inch or two. The second thought, and I guess it was what saved me for the third act, was—"This man isn't crazy; if he's a real homicidal maniac, then I'm Bill Shakespeare." And I'm not Bill Shakespeare, but I *do* have a strong sense of motivation, and that was the rub here. There *was* a motivation behind the visit of the chap with the scattergun who was about to use it to scatter my brains over Mac's carpet. I'd called him on it, and that was how I'd asked for trouble.

And I saw that the reason I was going to die, if I was, concerned that very question of whether or not he was crazy. He suspected now that I suspected he wasn't. My only chance was to convince him otherwise, and darned quick.

I started talking, and I didn't start out by accusing him of being batty — that would have been a giveaway of what I was trying to do. I talked fast, but I made my voice soft and calm and soothing, like Mac's had been when Mac was trying to talk him out of committing a couple of murders. I talked as though I were talking to a madman and was trying to calm him down.

"Listen," I told him, "you don't want to shoot me, Herman. I've never done anything to you, have I? Sure, I made a pass at you before, but that was because I thought you were going to kill Mac, and Mac's a friend of mine, Herman. A good friend. You can't blame me for that, can you?" Well, I went on from there, and I repeated myself with variations, and I guess I got it across. The gun stayed pointed at my head, but it didn't explode and I began to think that it wasn't going to.

Funny, come to think of it. Here was a guy who was either a homicidal maniac or he wasn't, and I felt convinced that if he thought I thought he was crazy, I'd get by. If he thought I saw through his act, as that incautious question of mine had indicated, I was a dead duck. And the only way to convince him that I was being hoodwinked, was to pretend I thought he was mad and was humoring him. So I humored him; I talked, believe me, I *talked.*

And then, abruptly, he grunted and stuck that scattergun through his belt. He took a large clasp knife from his pocket and opened a four-inch blade.

He reached down and grabbed a handful of my coatfront and dragged me across the carpet a couple of yards to where a square of bright moonlight came in the open window behind Mac's desk, and he held me so my head was in that moonlight, and —

MAD DOG! 43

I gave an involuntary yowl and began to almost wish he'd decided to use that scattergun after all. He took a handful of my hair in his left hand, and—sitting on my chest so I couldn't move—he turned my head around sidewise.

He put the knife down a moment and took hold of my left ear, bending down as though to examine it carefully. Then he let go and picked up the knife again. And I remembered what he'd been saying to Mac ten minutes or so ago—"The *ears,* Doc. Those damned ears—they—"

Was the guy crazy, or was he just trying to convince me that he was? I thought for a minute it was going to cost me an ear or two to find out. I howled, "Herman, don't—" and never knew until then just how eloquent I was.

Whether it was my eloquence or not, he decided at last that he didn't want my ears. He grunted and put the knife back in the pocket of that capacious overcoat. He said, "No good. They're not Wunderly."

He got up from my chest and started toward the door. He must have guessed that I was already wondering how soon it would be safe to yell for help. He turned back a minute and took a handkerchief out of his pocket. Then he said, "The hell with it. Yell all you want. Yell to the seagulls."

I watched the big dark shadow of him go through the doorway and I didn't say thanks or good-bye. I was going to let well enough alone. I heard his footsteps across the porch.

I didn't yell to the seagulls; he was right about that. Mac's place is a mile from its nearest neighbor, three miles from the coast guard station that has the only telephone on that part of the beach. And I didn't worry about trying to loosen my bonds; I'd found them too tough to handle even before he'd added to them with the heavy twine.

Mac was my—our—only chance of getting out of there in time to make a third act curtain. I crawled across, or rather wriggled my way across, to where he lay. He was breathing heavily now, and once as I worked my way toward him he moved a bit.

Probably he'd have snapped out of it quickly if I'd been able to give his face a few healthy slaps, but that wasn't possible. Fortunately he was lying on his side; I'd have had a devil of a job rolling him over if he'd been on his back where I couldn't get at the knots at his wrists.

I wriggled up behind him, and began work on those knots with my teeth. It was slow tough work, about the hardest thing I ever tackled. But I plugged along at it, and in between tries, I yelled at him and nudged him in the back with my head. Finally he said, "What happened, Bryce?"

"He's gone," I told him. "We're tied up. That's all. Listen, Mac, I'll keep on with these knots. If you can talk okay, tell me who the guy is and what's what, while I get you loose if I can."

His voice gradually got stronger as he talked. "Herman Wunderly," he told me. "Homicidal maniac, killed his sister several years ago. Gruesome business; cut off her ears. He's got some mania about ears.

"I was up here for the summer when it happened, and I helped handle him, and had to testify. The Wunderly place is a mile down the beach; nearest house here, in fact. They're year-rounders, residents, a bit eccentric. There's old man Wunderly now, and Herman's brother Kurt. He's going back to kill them unless we can—"

I'd got the knot loosened a bit now; it wouldn't be much longer. But my bruised and cut lip hurt so badly I had to stop for a second or two. I said, "Are they all as batty as Herman? Good Lord—sorricide, patricide—"

Then I went back to work on the knots. Mac said, "Neither. Herman and Kurt are brothers, but they were adopted. So Ethel wasn't their sister, and Old Man Wunderly isn't—"

Then the knot gave way, and Mac sat up, got his hands braced

MAD DOG! 45

on the edge of the desk, stood up and worked his way around it. I said, "Hey, how about me? Untie—"

"Scissors," he told me. "Quicker." He found them in a drawer, cut the cord from his ankles, and then cut me loose. "One of those neckties," I said, "was mine. And a new silk one at that. You owe me—"

"Shut up, you dope. Listen, you take the coast guard station, three miles northwest. Have 'em send men quick. I'll go to the Wunderlys', and maybe I'll be in time to—"

"Got another gun, Mac, besides the one he took?"

He shook his head. "Tell the coast guard boys to come armed. Don't worry about me; handling nuts is my business. I can take care of—"

I'd switched the light back on while he was talking, and I grinned at him. "So I noticed," I cut in. "Come on, if you're going."

He was going, all right. He was running so fast I had to yell the last of that remark after him. I ran after, using the forethought to grab up a fairly hefty cane that was in the umbrella rack in the corner of the hallway. I wasn't leaning on Mac's persuasive abilities with a homicidal maniac—nor counting on my own to work a second time.

I caught up with him and grabbed his arm. "You can't run a mile through sand," I yelled. "You'll fall down before you get half way—"

He saw the point in that and slowed down, and I panted alongside. "Our ears," I said. "We should have taken them off and left them back where they're safe."

"You're still drunk. Listen, be sensible and go back to the coast guard station and let me handle this. It isn't any of your business."

"They wouldn't get there in time and you know it and I'm not still drunk, dammit. And that second act stank, Mac. It needs doctoring, and I'm the guy who can—"

"Shut up, you sap. If you're going to come, save your breath for getting there."

It was good advice, and I took it.

He pushed on, sometimes running, sometimes walking—mostly according to the footing—and we were both fairly winded when we rounded the dune that hid the Wunderly house.

Mac said, "Shhh," and grabbed my arm. We were pretty close now, and he pointed to a window that was open about ten inches. We tiptoed to it, and got it open wider without making as much noise as I thought it would make.

The window was low enough that we could see in, and as far as we could tell looking into the darkened room, it was empty. Mac went in first, and I followed him. The room was just sufficiently illumined that we could make out where the furniture was, when our eyes had got accustomed to it.

Mac pointed toward one of the two closed doors and said, "Hallway. Stairs." And we crossed over and opened it. It didn't squeak, but the latch clicked when I let go the knob, and Mac grabbed my arm again, so hard and unexpectedly that I almost let out a yawp.

The hall was darker. I reached in my pocket for a box of matches, but Mac pulled me over to him and whispered in my ear, "I've been here. I know where the stairs are." He started off, feeling along the wall with one hand. I held on to the sleeve of his coat and followed.

We came to a turn, and he whispered, "This is the back of the staircase. Feel your way around it and you'll come to the bannister on the other side. We're going up."

"And then what?"

He answered, "Kurt and the old man sleep upstairs, and it looks like they've turned in early—unless we're too late. We'll see if they're all right first."

That sounded sensible. If they *were* all right, we'd have allies, and we could use them. And maybe there'd be a gun around. I still didn't feel very happy about chasing an armed maniac with only a walking stick for defense.

MAD DOG!

I whispered, "Listen —" and reached out for Mac.

But he'd moved on. I found the wall with my left hand and started to follow it around the staircase. Just around the corner, there was a door. A door there under the stairs meant a closet.

I don't know why I opened that door. I heard a faint rustling sound, or thought I did, inside the closet, as my hand went along the outside of the door. But I should have caught up with Mac and told him, and we should have done the thing cautiously. But I didn't wait. Like a fool, I jerked the door open.

For just a second there was so much light that I couldn't see a thing. Some closet doors are rigged like that — particularly closets off darkish hallways. When you open the door the light inside the closet goes on, and when you close it the light goes off again.

It's a handy arrangement, but I didn't appreciate it just then. That light seemed to flash right in my eyes, and it utterly blinded me. I heard an exclamation from Mac, who'd reached the foot of the stairs, and I heard another rustle in the closet and a noise that sounded like the growl of an animal.

For what was probably two seconds, but seemed two hours, I stood there blinking, and then I could see again.

I saw, back among the coats and things hanging in the closet, a tall figure in an outsize overcoat. Terrifyingly expressionless eyes stared at me out of a twisted face. And a familiar-looking scattergun pointed squarely at the pit of my stomach from a range of two feet or less.

It was one of those awful instants that seem to hang poised upon the brink of time's abyss interminably. There wasn't time for me to grab for that gun or jump sidewise from in front of its muzzle. But, as though in slow motion, I could see the knuckles of his hand whiten as his finger tightened on the trigger. I could see the hammer go back, hear the click as it slipped the pawl and see it start down toward the single chamber of the gun.

It clicked down—empty—and I was still standing there alive and without a hole blown through me and my liver splattered over the wall behind me. For another fraction of a second, I was too terrified to move. If that gun hadn't been loaded back at Mac's house, then this whole thing didn't make sense at all. But the guy who'd just pulled the trigger must have *thought* it was loaded or he wouldn't have pulled the trigger. Until he'd done that he had me buffaloed; I'd have put up my hands like a lamb with that thing looking at me. Add it up, and—

But the guy in the overcoat didn't wait to add it up. He came out of the closet after me in a flying leap like the charge of a tiger. The empty gun was raised now to be used as a bludgeon and just in the nick of time I got my cane up to block a blow that would have crushed my skull.

His wrist hit against the edge of the cane and the gun flew out of his hand, over my shoulder, and knocked a square foot of plaster out of the wall behind, before it hit the floor.

He kept on coming, though, and the momentum of his charge knocked me off my feet, and he was right there on top of me, his hands reached for my throat.

All this had happened before Mac could get back down the two or three steps of the staircase he'd started up, but I heard him yell, "Herman, stop!" and the thud of his feet as he vaulted over the bannister and came running.

One of Herman's hands had found my throat and I was having to use both my hands to keep the other one off when Mac got there. He joined the fray with a nifty full nelson that pulled the maniac's arms away from my throat and yanked him up to his knees. Then Mac let the full nelson slide to a half, and got one of Herman's arms pinned behind him in a hammerlock. It was neat work.

But all of this hadn't been accomplished in silence. Another light flashed on at the top of the stairs, and we heard slippered feet in the upper hallway.

MAD DOG! 49

"The old man?" I asked Mac.

"No, he's deaf; this wouldn't have waked him. That'll be Kurt Wunderly." He called out, "Hey, Wunderly. This is MacCready. Everything's under control, but come on down."

A tall man in a bathrobe thrown over pajamas was starting down the steps even before Mac finished talking. He said, "What on earth? Herman!"

Herman gave a yank to get free then, and I picked up the empty scattergun. Held by the barrel, it made a beautiful billy. I tapped Herman lightly on the skull—just a soft tap—and said, "Behave, sonny."

Mac was explaining to Kurt Wunderly. "Herman got away from the sanitarium. He was going to kill you and your fosterfather. Stopped at my place to brag about it or something, and left us tied up, but we—"

I said, "My name's Bryce. I was visiting—"

"The famous playwright?"

"Thanks," I said. "Better get us some ropes."

He nodded, his face a bit pale. "There should be some in the closet there." There were, and I got them.

I came in with the ropes. Herman made no resistance, his face was dull, expressionless, and his manner completely lethargic now. I'm no psychiatrist, but I recognized the symptoms of a manic-depressive insanity. Being captured had thrown him into the depressive state. Speechless, on the edge of sheer unconsciousness, he paid no attention to his surroundings or to what was said or done to him. Tying him up was routine. And old Mr. Wunderly turned out to be sleeping soundly, the sleep of the partly deaf, upstairs. Still with his ears on, so we didn't waken him.

Back down in the living room, Mac said, "Bryce and I will go to the coast guard station and phone for—"

"Hold it, Mac," I cut in. "I figured out what was wrong with that second act. Look," and I pointed at Herman, "this guy's crazy."

Mac gawped at me for a minute like he thought I was, too, and maybe he did just then.

I went on: "But your caller wasn't, Mac. He was pretending to be. Add that up." And I turned the scattergun around and pointed it at Kurt Wunderly, Herman's brother. I said, "Herman escaped and came here and asked you to protect him. He wasn't homicidal, just then. You hid him in that closet, and you came over to Mac's house to establish the idea that Herman was going to kill his foster-father and yourself. You turned out the light in Mac's study before you came in, and you figured that wearing that old overcoat and a hat and acting insane, you could pass for Herman in a darkened room.

"My guess is you wanted to kill Old Man Wunderly, probably because you thought he might live another ten years and you wanted your inheritance now. Or is that a good guess? Maybe you've got a taint of Herman's homicidal streak, too."

Mac cut in, "Bryce, do you realize what you're —"

"Pipe down, Mac," I told him, and went on talking to Kurt: "You left us tied up, ready to be witnesses that Herman was going to kill the old man. Then you came back here, gave him back the coat and gun, and you were getting into your pajamas when we came. Then you were going — except that we got here in time — to kill the old man and then 'capture' Herman and turn him over with the story that you'd overcome him after the first murder and while he was trying to kill you. He had nothing to lose by being blamed for another murder; he'd just be sent back. And who'd have believed anything he tried to tell them?"

Kurt Wunderly said, "That should make a good play, Mr. Bryce, but you're being absurd. Now put down that empty gun and —"

I laughed. "If you didn't know Herman was here, how do you know this gun is empty? Because you unloaded it before you gave it back to him, to play safe! You weren't in the hall when he clicked

MAD DOG! 51

it at me. You *couldn't* have known it was empty, if you're innocent."

I heard Mac give a low whistle.

I wanted to push the point home while I was at it, so I lied a little. My glimpse of the intruder's face in Mac's mirror had been too brief and too distant. But I said: "I can identify him, Mac. Before he reached around the corner in your study and turned out the light, I had a good look at his face in the mirror behind you—and his fingerprint will be on that light switch, and—"

The other proof came in a way I wasn't expecting. Kurt Wunderly yanked his hand out of his bathrobe pocket, and it held the thirty-two revolver that he'd taken away from Mac back at Mac's place.

He said, "You're too clever, Bryce. That forces me to go through with it—with one alteration. It will be found that Herman killed you and MacCready also."

I guess I began to sweat a little when I saw what I'd done. Mac and I were each maybe three yards from Kurt Wunderly, and not standing together. But if we tried to rush him, he'd be sure to get one of us. And this time he wasn't going to take any chances; I saw from his face that he was going to shoot us down here and now, and then take the time necessary to get the stage set before he went for help.

For some reason he picked Mac first—maybe to save me for last, I don't know. But he pointed the gun Mac's way, and said "Sorry, MacCready, but—" and I had to do something.

Just to stall an instant I said the first damn fool thing that popped into my head. I said, "It's a good thing I happened to have a shell to fit this scattergun, Wunderly. Drop your pistol!"

I knew as I said it that there wasn't a chance on earth that I'd be believed. People don't carry around small-gauge shotgun shells on the chance they'll find a gun to put them in. But it did divert his attention from Mac for the second. He swung the gun back my way.

The scattergun was hanging at my side and I brought it up as though to fire it. I saw Kurt Wunderly grin as he waited for the empty click that would call my bluff—before he shot me. But I didn't pull the trigger. I kept my hand arcing out with the gun in it, and let go of the gun, sailing it right at his face.

He triggered the revolver then and it spat noise and flame at me. But five pounds of cold steel being thrown into a man's face is enough to spoil his aim, even if he's easily able to duck the missile. That shot came close, undoubtedly, but it didn't hit me.

And Mac had leaped in the second he saw what I was doing, and had Kurt Wunderly by the wrist before he could fire again. I got there myself a split second later, and between us we had no trouble handling him. We tied him and put him on the couch beside Herman.

Mac went across to a decanter of whiskey on the buffet and poured himself a drink with a hand that shook just a trifle. He said, "Five minutes, and we'll go for help. How did you figure out—?"

"Playwright's instinct, Mac. I told you that second act just didn't jell, and you thought I was talking through my hat. But I know how I can *make* it jell. I got a dilly of an idea for that play I have to write. Listen, I start off with a lonely house and a homicidal—"

"Save it. I'll come down to New York and see it on the boards." He looked at the decanter of whiskey in his hand and then at me, incredulously. "Mean to say you're not having one with me?"

I shook my head firmly. "On the wagon till the play's complete. Or—say, I don't even *want* a drink. Mac, is there anything in this shock treatment of yours? And you didn't by any chance *arrange* all this just to—?"

He'd just downed the drink he'd poured—and he choked on it. When he could talk again he said, "You crazy—" and raised the decanter as though he was going to throw it at me. Then the reaction hit us, and we had an arm around each other's shoulders and laughed until it brought tears to our eyes.

HANDBOOK FOR HOMICIDE

The Road to Einar

It was raining like the very devil, and I couldn't see more than twenty feet ahead. The road was a winding mountain road, full of unexpected turns and dips apparently laid out by someone with more experience constructing roller coasters than highways.

Worse, it was soft gooey mud. I had to drive fast to keep from sinking in, and I had to drive slow to keep from going off the outer edge into whatever depth lay beyond.

They'd told me, forty miles back in Scardale, that I'd better not try to reach the Einar Observatory until the storm was over. And I was discovering now that they'd known what they were talking about.

Then, abruptly and with a remark I won't record, I slammed on the brakes. The car slithered to a stop and started to sink.

Dead ahead in the middle of the narrow road, right at the twenty-foot limit of my range of vision, was a twin apparition that resolved itself, as I slid to a stop five feet from it, into a man leading a donkey toward me.

There was a big wooden box on each side of the donkey, and there definitely wasn't going to be room for one of us to pass the other.

About twenty yards back behind me, I remembered, was a wider place in the road. But backward was uphill. I put the car into reverse and gunned the engine. The wheels spun around in the slippery mud, and sank deeper.

I cranked down the glass of the window and over the beat of the storm I yelled, "I can't back. How far behind you is a wider place in the road?"

The man shook his head without answering. I saw that he was an Indian, young and rather handsome. And he was magnificently wet.

Apparently he hadn't understood me, for a shake of the head wasn't any answer to my question. I repeated it.

"Two mile," he yelled back.

I groaned. If I had to wait while he led that donkey two miles back the way he had come, there went my chances of reaching Einar before dark. But he wasn't making any move to turn the beast around. Instead, he was untying the rope that held the wooden boxes in place.

"Hey, what's —" And then I realized that he was being smart, not dumb. The donkey, unencumbered by the load, could easily pass my car and could be reloaded on the other side.

He got one of the boxes off and came toward me with it. Alongside my car, he reached up and put it on the roof over my head.

I opened my mouth to object, and thought better. The box seemed light and probably wouldn't scratch the top enough to bother about.

Instead, I asked him what was in the boxes.

"Rattlesnakes."

"Good Lord," I said. "What for?"

"Sell 'em tourists — rattles, skins. Sell 'em venom drugstore."

"Oh," I said. And hoped the boxes wouldn't break or leak while they were on my car. A few loose rattlers in the back seat would be all I needed.

"Want buy big rattler? Diamondback? Cheap."

"No thanks," I told him.

He nodded, and led the donkey along the edge of nowhere past the car. Then he came back and got the boxes to reload on the donkey.

I yelled back, "Thanks!" and threw the shift into low. Downhill, it ought to start all right. But it didn't.

I opened the door and leaned out to look down at the wheels. They had sunk in up to the hubs.

The donkey, the rattlesnakes, and the Vanishing American were just starting off. I yelled.

The Indian came back. "Change 'em mind? Buy rattler?"

"Sorry, no. But could that creature of yours give this car a pull?"

He stared down at the wheels. "Plenty deep."

"It's headed downhill, though. And if I started the engine while he pulled, it ought to do it."

"Got 'em tow rope?"

"No, but you got the rope those boxes are tied with."

"Weak. No pull 'em."

"Five bucks," I said.

He nodded, went back to the donkey and untied the boxes. He put them down in the mud this time and tied the rope to my front bumper, looping it several thicknesses. Then he led the donkey back front and hitched it.

We tried for ten minutes—but the car was still stuck. I leaned out and yelled a suggestion: "Let the donkey pull while you rock the car."

We tried that. The wheels spun again, madly, and then caught hold. The car lurched forward suddenly—too suddenly—and what I should have foreseen happened. I slammed the brakes on, too late.

The donkey had stopped dead the minute the pull relaxed. The radiator of the car struck the creature's rump a glancing blow, and the donkey went over the edge. The car jerked sidewise toward the edge of the road, and there was a crackling sound as the rope broke.

Regardless of the knee-deep mud, I got out and ran to the edge.

The Indian was already there, looking down. He said, "It isn't deep here. But damn' it, I haven't got my gun along. Lend me your crank or a heavy wrench."

I hardly noticed the change in his English diction. I said, "I've got a revolver. Can you get down and up again?"

"Sure," he said. I got the revolver and handed it to him, and he went down. I could see him for the first few yards and then he was lost in the driving rain. There wasn't any shot, and in about ten minutes he reappeared.

"Didn't need it," he said, handing me back the pistol. "He was dead, poor fellow."

"What are you going to do now?" I asked him.

"I don't know. I suppose I'll have to stash those boxes and hike out."

"Look," I said, "I'm bound for the Einar Observatory. Come on with me, and you can get a lift from there back to town the first time a car makes the trip. How much was that donkey worth?"

"I'll take the lift," he said, "and thanks. But losing Archimedes was my own damn fault. I should have seen that was going to happen. Say, better get that car moving before it gets stuck again."

It was good advice and just in time. The car barely started. I kept it inching along while he tied the boxes on back and then got in beside me.

"Those boxes," I said. "Are they really rattlers, or was that off the same loaf as the Big Chief Wahoo accent?"

HANDBOOK FOR HOMICIDE 59

He smiled. "They're rattlesnakes. Sixty of them. Chap in Scardale starting a snake farm to supply venom to pharmaceutical labs hired me to round him up a batch."

"I hope the boxes are good and tight."

"Sure. They're nailed shut. Say, my name's Charlie Lightfoot."

"Glad to know you," I told him. "I'm Bill Wunderly. Going to take a job up at Einar."

"The hell," he said. "You an astronomer, or going on as an assistant?"

"Neither. Sort of an accountant-clerk. Wish I did know astronomy."

Yes, I'd been wishing that for several years now, ever since I'd fallen for Annabel Burke. That had been while Annabel was taking her master's degree in math, and writing her thesis on probability factors in quantum mechanics.

Heaven only knows how a girl with a face like Annabel's and a figure like Annabel's can possibly be a mathematics shark, but Annabel is.

Worse, she had the astronomy bug. She loved both telescopes and me, but I came out on the losing end when she chose between us. She'd taken a job as an assistant at Einar, probably the most isolated and inaccessible observatory in the country.

Then a month ago Annabel had written me that there was to be an opening at the observatory which would be within the scope of my talents.

I wrote a fervid letter of application, and now I was on my way to take the job. Nor storm nor mud nor dark of night nor boxes of rattlesnakes could stop me from getting there.

"Got a drink?" Charlie asked.

"In the glove compartment," I told him. "Sorry I didn't think to offer it. You're soaked to the skin."

He laughed. "I've been wet before and it hasn't hurt me. But I've been sober, and it has."

"You go to Haskell, Charlie?"

"No. Oxford. Hit hisn't the 'unting that 'urts the 'orse; hit's the 'ammer, 'ammer—"

"You're kidding me."

"No such luck." I heard the gurgle of liquid as he tilted the bottle. Then he added, "Oil. Pop's land."

I risked an unbelieving look out of the corner of my eye. Charlie's face was serious.

He said, "You wonder why I hunt rattlesnakes. For one reason, I like it, and for another— Well, if this was a quart instead of a pint, I could show you."

"But what happened to the oil money?"

"Pop's still got it. But the third time I went to jail, I stopped getting any of it. Not that I blame him. Say, take it easy down this hill. The bridge at the bottom was washed out four years ago, last time there was a big storm like this one."

But the bridge was still there, with the turbid waters of a swollen stream swirling almost level with the plank flooring. I held my breath as we went across it.

"It'll be gone in an hour," Charlie said, "if it keeps raining this hard. You haven't another bottle of that rye, have you?"

"No, I haven't. How do you catch rattlers, Charlie?"

"Pole with a loop of thin rope running through a hole in the end. Throw the loop over a snake and pull the loop tight. Then you can ease the pole in and grab him by the back of the neck."

"How about the ones you don't see?"

"They strike. But I wear thick shoes and I've got heavy leather leggings under my trousers. They never strike high, so I'm safe as long as I stay upright on level ground." He chuckled. "You ought to hear the sound of them striking those puttees. When you step in a nest of them, it sounds like rain on a tin roof."

I shivered a little, and wished I hadn't asked him.

Then, ahead of us, there were lights.

Charlie said, "Take the left turn here. You might as well drive right up to the garage."

I turned left, around the big dome on the north end of the building. Apparently, someone had heard us coming or seen our headlights, for the garage doors were opening.

I said, "You know the place, Charlie?"

"Know it?" His voice sounded surprised. "Hell, Bill, I designed it."

The Thud of Murder

Annabel was more beautiful than I had remembered her. I wanted to put my arms around her then and there, despite the presence — in the hallway with us — of Charlie Lightfoot and a morose-looking man in overalls, who'd let me in the garage and then led us into the main building.

But I had a hunch I wouldn't get away with it, besides I was standing in the middle of a puddle of water and was as wet as though I'd been swimming instead of driving.

Annabel looked fresh and cool and dry in a white smock. She said, "You should have waited in Scardale, Bill. I'm surprised you made it. Hello, Charlie."

Charlie said, "Hi, Annabel. I guess Bill's in safe hands now, so I'm going to borrow some dry clothes. See you later."

He left us, managing somehow to walk as silently as a shadow despite the heavy, wet shoes he was wearing.

Annabel turned to the man in overalls. "Otto, will you take Mr. Wunderly to his room?"

He nodded and started off, and I after him. But Annabel said, "Just a minute, Bill. Here's Mr. Fillmore."

A tall, saturnine man who had just come in one of the doorways held out his hand. "Glad to know you, Wunderly. Annabel's been talking about you a lot. I'm sure you're just the man we need."

I said, "Thanks. Thanks a lot." I guess I was thanking him mostly for telling me that Annabel had talked a lot about me.

I remembered, now, having heard of him. Fergus Fillmore, the lunar authority.

A minute later I followed the janitor up a flight of stairs and was shown to the room which was henceforth to be mine. I lost no time getting rid of my wet clothes and into dry ones. Then I hurried back downstairs.

A bridge game was in progress in the living room. Annabel and Fergus Fillmore were partners. Their opponents were a handsome young man and a rather serious-looking young woman who wore shell-rimmed glasses.

Annabel introduced them.

"Zoe, this is Mr. Wunderly. Bill, Miss Fillmore. . . . And Eric Andressen. He's an assistant, as I am."

Andressen grinned. "This is an experiment, Wunderly. Annabel thinks she can apply Planck's constant h to a tenace finesse."

There was a cheerful crackling fire in the fireplace. I stood with my back to it, behind Annabel's chair. But I didn't watch the play of the hand; I was too interested in studying the people I had just met.

Eric Andressen had a young, eager face and was darkly handsome. He could not have been more than a few years out of college. Something in his voice — although his English was perfect — made me think that college had been across the pond. Scandinavian, probably, as his name would indicate.

Zoe Fillmore, playing opposite Andressen, looked quite a bit like her father. She was attractive without being pretty. She seemed much less interested in the game than the others.

She caught me looking at her and smiled. "Would you care to take my hand after this deal, Mr. Wunderly? I'm awfully poor at cards. I don't know why they make me play."

While I was trying to decide whether to accept her offer, a

HANDBOOK FOR HOMICIDE 63

man I had not yet met came into the room. He said, "You were right, Fillmore. I blink-miked that corner of the plates again and—"

Fergus Fillmore interrupted him. "You found it, then? Well, never mind the details. Paul, this is Bill Wunderly, our new office man. Wunderly, Paul Bailey, our other assistant."

Bailey shook hands. "Glad to know you, Wunderly. I've heard a lot about you from Annabel. If you're as good as she says you are—"

Annabel looked flustered. She said, "Bill, this sounds like a conspiracy. Really, I haven't talked about you quite as much as these people would lead you to think."

Fillmore said, "Zoe has just offered Wunderly her hand, Paul. Would you care to take mine?"

Bailey's voice was hesitant. As though groping for an excuse, he said, "I'd like to—but—"

He paused, and, in the silence of that pause, there was a dull thud overhead.

We looked at one another across the bridge table. Bailey said, "Sounds like someone—uh—fell. I'll run up and see." He ran out the door that led to the hallway and we heard his swift footsteps thumping up the stairs.

There was an odd, expectant silence in the room. Eric Andressen had a card in his hand ready to play but held it.

We heard Bailey's footsteps overhead, heard him try a door and then rap on it lightly. Then he came down the stairs two steps at a time. Andressen and Fillmore were on their feet by now, crossing the room toward the doorway when Bailey appeared there.

His face was pale and in it there was a conflict of emotions that was difficult to read. Consternation seemed to predominate.

He said breathlessly, "My door's bolted from the inside. And it sounded as though what we heard came from there. I'm afraid we'll have to—"

"You mean somebody's *in* your room?" Zoe's voice was incredulous.

Her father turned and spoke to her commandingly. "You remain here, Zoe. And will you stay with her, Annabel?"

Obviously, he was taking command. He said to me, "You'd better come along, Wunderly. You're the huskiest of us and we might need you. But we'll try a hammer first, to avoid splintering the door. Will you get one, Eric?"

All of us, except Eric—who went into the kitchen for a hammer—went up the stairs together. Almost as soon as we'd reached Bailey's door, Andressen came running up with a heavy hammer.

Fergus Fillmore turned the knob and held it so the latch of the door was open. He showed Andressen where to hit with the hammer to break the bolt. On Eric's third try, the door swung open.

Bailey and Fillmore went into the room together. I heard Bailey gasp. He hurried toward a corner of the room. Then Andressen and I went through the doorway.

The body of a young woman with coppery red hair lay on the floor.

Bailey was bending over her. He looked up at Fillmore. "She's *dead!* But I don't understand how—?"

Fillmore knelt, looked closely at the dead girl's face, gently lifted one of her eyelids and studied the pupil of the eye. He ran exploratory fingers around the girl's temples and into her hair. Turning her head slightly to one side, he felt the back of the skull.

Then he stood up, his eyes puzzled. "A hard blow. The bone is cracked and a portion of it pressed into the brain. It seems hard to believe that a fall—"

Bailey's voice was harsh. "But she *must* have fallen. What else could have happened? That window's locked and the door was bolted from the inside."

Eric Andressen said slowly, "Paul, the floor's carpeted. Even if she fell rigidly and took all her weight on the back of the head, it would hardly crack the skull."

Paul Bailey closed his eyes and stood stiffly, as though with a physical effort he was gathering himself together. He said, "Well — I suppose we'd better leave her as she is for the moment. Except —" He crossed to the bed on the other side of the room and pulled off the spread, returned and placed it over the body.

Andressen was staring at the inside of the door. "That bolt could be pulled shut from the outside, easily, with a piece of looped string. Look here, Fillmore."

He went out into the hall and the rest of us followed him. At the second door beyond Bailey's room, he turned in. In a moment he returned with a piece of string.

He folded it in half and put the fold over the handle of the small bolt, then with the two ends in his hand he came around the door. He said, "Will you go inside, Wunderly? So you can open the door again, if this works. No use having to break my bolt, too."

I went inside and the door closed. I saw the looped string pull the bolt into place. Then, as Andressen let go one end of it and pulled on the other, the string slid through the crack of the door.

I rejoined the others in the hallway. Bailey's face was white and strained. He said, "But *why* would anyone want to kill Elsie?"

Andressen put his hand on Bailey's shoulder. He said, "Come on, Paul. Let's go find Lecky. It'll be up to him, then, whether to notify the police."

When they'd left, I asked Fergus Fillmore, "Who is — was — Elsie?"

"The maid, serving-girl. Lord, I hope I'm wrong about that head-wound being too severe to be accounted for by a fall. There's going to be a bad scandal for the observatory, if it's murder."

"Were she and Paul Bailey — ?"

"I'm afraid so. And it's pretty obvious Paul knew she was

waiting for him in his room. When he heard that thud downstairs, you remember how Paul acted."

I nodded, recalling how Bailey had hurried upstairs before anyone else could offer to investigate. And how he'd gone directly to his own room, not looking into any of the adjacent ones.

Fillmore said, "Mind holding the fort here till Lecky comes? I'm going down to send Zoe home."

"Home?" I asked. "Doesn't she live here?"

"Our house is a hundred yards down the slope, next to Lecky's. There are three houses outside the main building, for the three staff members. Everyone else lives in the main building."

When Fillmore had left I walked to the window at the end of the hallway. The storm outside had stopped—but the one inside was just starting.

Bailey and Andressen returned with a short, bald-headed, middle-aged man. Abel Lecky, the director.

He and the others turned into Bailey's room and I went back downstairs.

Annabel was alone in the room in which the bridge game had been going on. She stood up as I came in. "Bill, Fergus tells me that Elsie's dead. He took his daughter on home. But how—?"

I told her what little I knew.

"Bill," she said, "I'm afraid. Something's been wrong here. I've felt it."

I put my hands on her shoulders.

She said, "I'm—I'm glad you're here, Bill." She didn't resist or push me away when I kissed her but her lips were cool and passive.

The Murderer's Guide

There were heavy footsteps. Annabel and I stepped apart just as the door opened. A short, very fat man wearing a lugubrious expression came into the room. Pince-nez spectacles seemed grotesquely out of place on his completely round face.

He said, "Hullo, Annabel. And I suppose this is your wonderful Wunderly." Without giving either of us a chance to speak, he held out his hand to me and kept on talking. "Glad to know you, Wunderly. I'm Hill. Darius Hill. Annabel, what's wrong with Zoe? I passed her and Fillmore out in the hall. She looked as though she'd seen ghillies and ghosties."

Annabel said, "Elsie Willis is dead, Darius."

"Elsie *dead?* You're fooling me, Annabel. Why, I saw her only a few hours ago, and— Could it have been *murder?*"

The italics were his. He took off his pince-nez glasses and his eyes went as round as his face.

I said, "Nobody knows, Mr. Hill. It might have been accidental. Probably she fainted and fell."

"Fainted? A buxom wench like Elsie?" He shook his head vigorously. "But—you say fell? That would imply a head injury, would it not? Of course.

"But what a banal method of murder—with a garage full of rattlesnakes at hand. And with Bailey a chemist, too. Or would Zoe have done it? I fear she would be inclined to direct and unimaginative methods but I didn't think she harbored any animosity—"

"Please, Mr. Hill." Annabel's voice was sharp and I noticed she addressed him by his last name this time, not his first. "If it was murder, neither Paul nor Zoe could have done it. They were both in this room, right here, when she died. We all heard her fall."

"Ah—then the scene of the crime was upstairs? And right over this room. Let's see—of course. She was in Bailey's room, waiting for him."

"Apparently. Paul had been sent to check plates on the blink-mike and he was passing through here on his way to his room when—when it happened. If you'll both pardon me, I think I'd better go tell the housekeeper about it. She should know right away."

Hill and I both nodded. Hill said, "I'd like to talk to you, Wunderly. Come on up to my room and have a drink.

"This way—" He was taking my acceptance for granted, so I could do nothing but follow.

Hill's room was just like the one that had been assigned to me, save that one entire side of it was made up of shelves of books.

While he hunted for the bottle and glasses, I strolled to the shelves and looked them over. The books were in haphazard order and they concerned, as far as I could see, only three subjects; one of which didn't fit at all with the other two. Astronomy, mathematics—and criminology.

When I turned around, Hill had poured drinks for us. He waved me to a chair, saying:

"And now you will tell me about the murder."

He listened closely, interrupting several times with pertinent questions.

When I had finished, he chuckled. "You are a close observer, Wunderly. If I am to solve this case, I shall let you be my Watson."

"Or your Archie?"

He laughed aloud. *"Touche!* I grant more resemblance, physically at least, to Nero Wolfe than to the slender Holmes."

He sipped his drink thoughtfully for a moment, then said, "I'm quite serious, though, about solving it. As you've undoubtedly deduced from your examination of my library, murder is my hobby. Not committing murder, I assure you, but studying it. I consider murder—the toss of a monkeywrench into the wheels of the infinite—the most fascinating of all fields of research.

"Yes, I shall most certainly take full advantage of the fact that someone has, figuratively, left a corpse conveniently in my very back yard."

I said, "But if you're serious about investigating shouldn't you—"

"Study the scene of the crime and the *corpus delicti?* Not at all, my dear boy. I assure you that I am much more likely to reach the truth listening to the sound of my own voice than by looking at dead young women."

"Why do you think that?"

"Isn't it obvious? A kills B—or rather, in this case, X kills *Elsie*. One could pun with the formula X kills LC, but that is irrelevant, not to say irreverent. My point is—would he leave her body in such a manner that looking at it would inform the looker who killed her? Of course not, and if a calling card is found under the body, it might or might not be that of the murderer. . . . What do you think of Andressen?"

"Eric?" The sudden question surprised me. "Why, I hardly know him. Seems likable enough. He's Norwegian, isn't he?"

"Yes. He plays cello, too. Not badly. A brilliant, if erratic chap. How do you like Fergus Fillmore?"

"I like him well enough. His main interest is the moon, isn't it?"

"Right. Good old Luna, goddess of the sky. Thinks the others of us waste our time with distant galaxies and nebulae. How about another drink, Wunderly?"

"Thanks, no," I told him. "I think I'd better look up Annabel. She—"

"Nonsense. You're going to see plenty of Annabel from now on. Right now we're talking about murder, or had we digressed? Are you interested in murder, by the way?"

"Not personally. Oh, I like to read a good murder mystery but—"

"Murder mysteries? Bah, there's no mystery in them. A clever reader can always guess the murderer. I ought to know; I read them by the dozens. One simply ignores the clues and analyzes the author's manner of presenting the characters.

"No, Wunderly, I'm talking about real murder. It's fascinating. I'm writing a book on the subject. Call it 'The Murderer's Guide'. If I say so myself—it is excellent. Superb, in fact."

"I'd like to read it."

"Oh, you shall, you shall. It will be difficult for you to avoid reading it, I assure you. Here is the manuscript to date—first fifteen chapters and there are two more to be written. Take it along with you."

I took the thick sheaf of typed manuscript hesitantly. "But do you want to part with it for a day or two? I doubt if I'll have time to read it tonight, so may I not borrow it later instead?"

"Take it along. No hurry about returning it. Leave it in your room and go seek your Annabel. Later, if you're not sleepy, you might want to read a chapter or two before you turn in. Possibly you'll read something that will come in handy within the next few days."

"Thanks," I said and stood up, glad to be dismissed. "But what do you mean about the next few days?"

"The next murder, of course. You don't think Elsie is going into the great unknown all by herself, do you? Think it over, and you'll see what I mean. Who is Elsie to deserve being murdered? A scullery maid with red hair and willing disposition. Nobody would want to kill Elsie!"

"But unless it was an accidental death after all," I said, a bit bewildered by this point of view, "somebody *did* kill her."

"Exactly. That proves my point. The death of a scullery maid would scarcely be the real desideratum of the murderer, would it?"

In my room, I put the manuscript down on the desk and leafed it open to a random paragraph. I was curious merely to see whether Darius Hill's style of writing matched his brand of conversation.

"The murderer," I read, *"who is completely ruthless has the best chance of evading detection. By ruthless I mean willing to kill without strong motive*

which can be traced back to him, or, better still, without motive at all other than the desire to confuse.

"Adequate motive is the murderer's bête noire. *The mass murderer, who lacks in each crime adequate motive therefor, is less vulnerable to suspicion than the murderer of a single victim through whose death he benefits.*

"It is for this reason that the clever murderer, rather than the stupid one, is led from crime to crime. . . ."

There was a rap on my door. I said, "Come in."

Eric Andressen opened the door. "Annabel's looking for you. Thought you'd want to know."

"Thanks," I told him. "I'll be right down. Hill just loaned me the manuscript of his book, by the way. Have you read it?"

He grinned wryly. "Everybody here who can read has read it. And those who can't read have had it read *to* them."

I flicked off my light and joined him in the hallway. I asked, "Have the police arrived?"

"The police won't be here," said Andressen grimly. "The bridge is gone. Phone wires are down, too, but we notified them by shortwave. There's a two-way set here."

I whistled softly. "Are we completely cut off, or is there another way around?"

"Yes, over the mountains, but it would take days. Be quicker to wait till they send men out from Scardale to replace the bridge. The stream will be down by tomorrow night."

Seven Times Death

Fergus Fillmore was just leaving the main room downstairs when I entered. Lecky, the director, looking austere and thoughtful, was standing in front of the fireplace.

I heard Fillmore say, "Here's Eric back. He and I can manage Elsie between us. And if you can think of something for Paul Bailey to do, he'll be better off out of the way."

Lecky nodded. "Tell him I said to go to my office and wait for me there."

"Come on, Eric," Fillmore said to Andressen. "Get your flashbulbs and camera. We'll take pictures before we move the body."

"All right. Where are we — uh — going to put her?"

"We'll use the crate that the cylinder of the star-camera came in. We can turn it into a makeshift sort of refrigerator with some tubing and Rex's help. We'll borrow this refrigerating unit out of the—"

Their conversation faded as they went up the steps.

Director Lecky said, "An unfortunate evening, Wunderly. I'm afraid you're not getting much of a welcome but we're glad you're here."

"When shall I start on my duties, sir?"

"Don't worry about that. Take a day or two to familiarize yourself with the place and get to know the people you'll work with. Work is light here anyway, in bad weather."

"Shall I help Fillmore and Andressen?" I suggested.

"They'll do all right. Andressen's a bug on photography; got enough equipment to set up as a professional. And Rex Parker will have the refrigeration ready for them when they're ready for it. Have you met Rex?"

"No. Is he another of the assistants?"

"He's our electrician-mechanic. But — Lord, I nearly forgot to tell you. Annabel went up on the roof and you're to join her there. In fact, I've delegated her to show you around."

I found Annabel looking out over the parapet at the edge of the roof. Following her gaze, I saw a jagged, rocky landscape. Here and there one could catch glimpses of the tortuous turnings of the swollen stream.

She asked, "Did Darius talk an arm off you, Bill?"

"It was dangling by a shred," I told her. "He gave me the manuscript of his book to read."

"That book!" Annabel said. "It's horrible; let's not talk about it. Darius is a bit of a bore, but he really isn't as bad as that book would lead you to believe."

"It's hardly bedtime reading," I admitted. "But I've a hunch I'm going to find it interesting. Annabel—"

"Now, Bill, don't start talking in *that* tone of voice. Not tonight, anyway. Look, there's the dome down at that end of the building. Tomorrow I'll show you around inside it. It's—"

"Sixty feet high," I said, "and houses the thirty-inch telescope, which is forty-six feet long. The dome is movable and the floor is a great elevator whose motion enables the observer to follow the eyepiece of the telescope without climbing ladders. I've read all about it, so let's talk about us."

"Not tonight, Bill, please."

"All right." I sighed. "But I'm more interested in people than telescopes. Have I met everyone? Or let's put it this way: I've heard about a few people I haven't met; a housekeeper, a cook, and an electrician named Rex something. Are there any others?"

"Parker is Rex's last name. I guess that's all of us except a handy man who helps Otto the janitor. You met Otto. And—oh, yes, there's Mrs. Fillmore and Mrs. Lecky; you haven't met either of them. Neither were over at the main building tonight. And there's a stenographer who'll help you, but she's away on sick leave."

"The three astronomers live in separate houses?"

"Lecky and Fillmore do. There's another house for the third staff member, but it's vacant because Darius Hill is a bachelor and doesn't want to live in it alone. So he rooms in, like the rest of us."

I counted on my fingers. "Three astronomers; Lecky, Fillmore, Hill. Three assistants; Paul Bailey, Eric Andressen, and you. Rex Parker, Otto the janitor, and a handy man. Housekeeper, cook, wives of two astronomers and daughter of one. Fifteen of us here, if I counted right."

"And Charlie Lightfoot. Not a resident but he drops in often."

"Sixteen people," I said, "and sixty rattlesnakes. I hope *they* don't drop in often. Say, about Paul Bailey. Is he—"

I never finished that question, for from somewhere below us, and outside the building, came the sound of a scream.

There is something more frightening in the scream of a man than that of a woman. Possibly it is because men, in general, scream less often and, in most cases, only with greater cause.

At any rate, I felt a tingling sensation on my scalp—as though my hair were rising on end. Annabel and I ran to the parapet on the south end of the building and looked down.

A man was running from the garage, screaming as he ran.

We heard a door of the main building jerk open and slam shut. Then Annabel and I were hurrying for the stairs that led down from the roof.

"It was Otto," she gasped. "Do you suppose that a snake—?"

That was just what I did suppose and I didn't like to think about it. Because it was very unlikely that *one* snake had got loose—and there were thirty in each box.

We pounded down the stairs and ran along the hallway. A man in dungarees and a blue denim shirt almost collided with me. I guessed him to be Parker, the electrician.

He hurried past us. "Stay out of there, Miss Burke. Charlie's ripping Otto's clothes off. I'm getting ammonia." Then he was past us.

I said, "Wait in the living room, Annabel. I'll see if I can help Charlie."

I shoved her firmly through the door of the living room. Not because I shared Parker's prudishness but because I had in mind doing something Annabel would probably object to my doing.

From the roof I had seen that Otto had left the garage door open. That door wouldn't be visible from the windows here and the others wouldn't know about it. That door should be closed.

I pushed through into the kitchen.

Otto was stretched out on the floor there. Fergus Fillmore and the cook held him down, while Charlie Lightfoot worked on him.

HANDBOOK FOR HOMICIDE

About each of Otto's legs, high on the thigh, Charlie had tied a makeshift tourniquet.

Now he was busy with a sharp knife, using it with the cool precision of a surgeon. I could see that there were several gashes from that knife in each leg.

No one paid any attention to me as I sidled past. I looked out through the pane of the door, and there was moonlight enough in the yard for me to see something I didn't like at all — high grass.

But I opened the door and slipped out, closing it quickly behind me. If I hurried, maybe I could get that garage door shut in time.

I held my breath as I headed for the garage building. My eyes strained against the dimness and my ears against the silence of the night, my muscles alert to leap back at the first sound of a rattle.

I'd almost made the garage before I heard it. A five-foot rattler had been coming through the open doorway. He coiled and rattled.

I froze where I stood, six feet from him. I knew he wouldn't be able to reach me from where he was; no rattlesnake can strike farther than two-thirds of his own length.

Keeping a good distance from him, I began to circle around to put the open door between us. Now I was in double danger, for my course took me off the path and into the high grass. If other snakes had already come out of the garage, I'd probably step on one without seeing it.

But I didn't; I got behind the door and I threw myself forward against it and slammed it shut.

I'd have been safer walking back to the main building but I ran instead. Even running, it seemed as though it took me thirty minutes to cover the thirty steps to the kitchen door.

Then I was safe inside.

"Couldn't do a thing," Charlie was saying. "Seven bites — and one of them — *that* one — hit a vein. They die in three minutes, when the fangs hit a vein."

Otto was lying very still now.

Rex Parker burst in the door, a glass in one hand and a bottle in the other. "The ammonia. One teaspoonful in — Oh! Too late?"

Charlie Lightfoot stood up slowly. He saw me and his eyes widened.

"Bill, you look as though — Good Lord! I remember now I heard that door closing. Did you go out in the yard?"

I nodded and leaned back against the door behind me. Reaction had left me weak as a kitten.

"He left the garage door open," I told them. "We saw that from the roof. I closed it."

"You didn't get bit?"

"No." I saw a bottle of whiskey on the table and crossed unsteadily toward it to pour myself a drink. But my hand shook and Charlie took the bottle from me. He poured a stiff shot and handed it to me.

He said, "You got guts, Wunderly."

I shook my head. "Other way around. Too damn afraid of snakes to have slept if I'd known there were a lot of them around loose."

I felt better when I'd downed the shot.

Charlie Lightfoot said, "I'll have to go out there and count noses, as soon as I get my puttees back on."

Parker said, "Are you sure it isn't too—"

"I'll be safe enough, Rex. Get me a flashlight or a lantern, though."

Fillmore's voice sounded wobbly. "We'll have to take care of Otto's body like we took care of Elsie's. Wunderly, will you tell Andressen to come help me?"

"Sure. Is he in his room?"

Fillmore nodded. "Listen. That's his cello."

I listened and realized now, as one can realize and remember afterwards, that I had heard it all along—from the moment Annabel and I had come through the doorway passage from the roof.

I asked, "Shall I look up Dr. Lecky, too?"

"He went over to his house," Fillmore said. "I'll call him on the house phone. It's still working, isn't it, Rex?"

Parker nodded. "Sure. But look, Mr. Fillmore, better tell Lecky not to try to come over here. There may be rattlers loose around outside, even if the door did get shut before most of them got out."

Charlie Lightfoot put down the whiskey bottle. "Hell, yes. Tell him within half an hour I'll know how many are at large, if any. And Fillmore, how about your wife and daughter? Is there any chance either of them would go out of the house tonight? If so, you better warn them."

"I'll do that, Charlie. They're both in for the night. But I'll phone and make sure."

I went to the living room first, told Annabel what had happened and told her I was going up to get Andressen.

She said, "I'm going upstairs, too. I think I'll turn in."

"Excellent idea," I told her.

I left Annabel at the turn of the corridor, with a kiss that made my lips tingle and my head spin.

"Be sure," I whispered, "that you lock and bolt your door tonight. And don't ask me why. I don't know."

Andressen was playing Rimsky-Korsakoff's *Coq D'Or*. A pagan hymn to the sun that seemed a strange choice for an astronomer.

My knock broke off the eerie melody. The bow was still in his hand when he opened the door.

"Otto Schley is dead, Eric," I told him. "Fillmore wants your help."

Without asking any questions, he tossed the bow down on the bed and flicked off the light switch.

"About Mr. Hill and Paul Bailey," I asked. "Do you know where they are?"

"Bailey's probably asleep. He had a spell of the jitters, so Darius and I gave him a sedative—and we made it strong. Darius is probably in his room."

He hurried downstairs, and I went on along the corridor to Darius Hill's room and knocked on the door.

He called out, "Come in, Wunderly."

A Toast to Fear

I closed the door behind me, and asked curiously, "How did you know who it was?" Hill's chuckle shook his huge body. He snapped shut the book he had been reading and put it down on the floor beside his morris chair. Then he looked up at me.

"Simple, my dear Wunderly. I heard your voice and that of Eric. One of you goes downstairs, the other comes here. It would hardly be Eric; he dislikes me cordially. Besides, he has been in his room playing that miserable descendant of the huntsman's bow. So I take it that you came to tell him, and then me, about the second murder."

I stared at him, quite likely with my mouth agape.

Darius Hill's eyes twinkled. "Come, surely you can see how I know that. My ears are excellent, I assure you. I heard that scream—even over the wail of the violincello. It was a man's voice. I'm not sure, but I'd say it was Otto Schley. Was it?"

I nodded.

"And it came from the approximate direction of the garage. There are rattlesnakes in the garage. Or there were."

"There are," I said. "Probably fewer of them." I wished I knew that. "But why did you say it was murder?" I asked him. "Loose rattlesnakes are no respecters of persons."

"Under the circumstances, Wunderly, do *you* think it was an accident?"

HANDBOOK FOR HOMICIDE 79

"Under what circumstances?"

Darius Hill sighed. "You are being deliberately obtuse, my young friend. It is beyond probability that two accidental deaths should occur so closely spaced, among a group of seventeen people living in non-hazardous circumstances."

"Sixteen people," I corrected.

"No, seventeen. I see you made a tabulation but that it was made after Elsie's death so you didn't count her. But if you figure it that way, you'll have to deduct one for Otto and call it fifteen. There are now fifteen living, two dead."

"If you heard that scream, why didn't you go downstairs? Or did you?"

"I did not. There were able bodied men down there to do anything that needed doing. More able-bodied, I might say, than I. I preferred to sit here in quiet thought, knowing that sooner or later someone would come to tell me what happened. As you have done."

The man puzzled me. Professing an interest in crime, he could sit placidly in his room while murders were being done, lacking the curiosity to investigate at first hand.

He pursed his lips. "You countered my question with another, so I'll ask it again. Do you think Schley's death was accidental?"

I answered honestly. "I don't know what to think. There hasn't been time to think. Things happened so—"

His dry chuckle interrupted me. "Does not that answer your question as to why I stayed in this room? You rushed downstairs and have been rushing about ever since, without time to think. I sat here quietly and thought. There was nothing I could learn downstairs that I cannot learn now, from you. Have a drink and tell all."

I grinned, and reached for the bottle and glass. The more I saw of Darius Hill, the less I knew whether I liked him or not. I believed that I could like him well enough if I took him in sufficiently small doses.

"Shall I pour one for you?" I asked him.

"You may. An excellent precaution, Wunderly."

"Precaution?" I asked. "I don't understand."

"Did I underestimate you? Too bad. I thought you suspected the possibility of my having poisoned the whiskey in your absence. It is quite possible—as far as you know—that I am the murderer. And that you are the next victim."

He picked up the glass I handed to him and held it to the light. "Caution, in a situation like this, is the essence of survival. Will you trade glasses with me, Wunderly?"

I looked at him closely to see whether or not he was serious. He was.

He said, "You turned to the bureau to pour this. Your back was toward me. It is possible— You see what I mean?"

Yes, he was dead serious. And, staring at his face, I saw something else that I had not suspected until now. The man was frightened. Desperately frightened.

And, suddenly, I realized what was wrong with Darius Hill.

I brought a clean glass and the whiskey bottle from the bureau and handed it to him. I said, "I'll drink both the ones I poured, if I may. And you may pour yourself a double one to match these two."

Gravely, Darius Hill filled the glass from the bottle.

"A toast," I said and clinked my glass to his. "To necrophobia."

Glass half upraised to his lips, he stared at me. He said, "Now I *am* afraid of you. You're clever. You're the first one that's guessed."

I hadn't been clever, really. It was obvious, when one put the facts together. Darius Hill's refusal to go near the scene of a crime, despite his specialization in the study of murder—in theory.

Necrophobia; fear of death, fear of the dead. The very depth of that fear would make murder—on paper—a subject of morbid and abnormal fascination for him.

To some extent, his phobia accounted for his garrulity; he

HANDBOOK FOR HOMICIDE

talked incessantly to cover fear. And he made himself deliberately eccentric in other directions so that the underlying cause of his true eccentricity would be concealed from his colleagues.

We drank. Darius Hill, very subdued for the first time since I'd met him, suggested another. But the double one had been enough for me. I declined, and left him.

In the corridor I heard the bolt of his door slide noisily home into its socket.

I headed for my own room but heard footsteps coming up the stairs. It was Charlie coming down the hallway toward me. His face look gaunt and terrible. What would have been pallor in a white man made his face a grayish tan.

He saw me and held out his right hand, palm upward. Something lay in it, something I could not identify at first. Then, as he came closer, I saw that it was the rattle from a rattlesnake's tail.

He smiled mirthlessly. "Bill," he said, "Lord help the astronomers on a night like this. Somebody's got a rattlesnake that won't give warning before it strikes. Better take your bed apart tonight before you get into it."

"Come in and talk a while," I suggested, opening my door.

Charlie Lightfoot shook his head. "Be glad to talk, but let's go up on the roof. I need fresh air. I feel as though I'd been pulled through a keyhole."

"Sure," I said, "but first shall we —"

"Have a drink?" he finished for me. "We shall not. Or rather, I shall not. That's what's wrong with me at the moment, Bill. Sobering up."

We were climbing the steps to the roof now. Charlie opened the door at the top and said, "This breeze feels good. May blow the alky fumes out of my brain. Look at that dome in the moonlight, will you? Looks like a blasted mosque. Well, why not? An observatory is a sort of mosque on the cosmic scale, where the devotees worship Betelgeuse and Antares, burning parsecs for incense and chanting litanies from an ephemeris."

"Sure you're sober?" I asked him.

"I've got to be sober; that's what's wrong. I was two-thirds pie-eyed when Otto— Say, thanks for closing that garage door. You kept most of them in. I didn't dare take time to go out, because of Otto."

I asked, "Was it murder, Charlie? Or could the box have come apart accidentally if Otto moved it?"

"Those boxes were nailed shut, Bill. Someone took the four nails out of the lid of one of them, with a nail-puller. Then the box was stood on end leaning against the door, with the lid on the under side and the weight of the box holding the lid on. Otto must have heard it fall when he went in but must not have guessed what it was."

"How many of the snakes did you find?"

"You kept seventeen of them in the garage when you slammed the door. I got two more in the grass near the door. That leaves eleven that got away, and I'll have to hunt for them as soon as it's light. That's why I've got to sober up. And, dammit, sobering up from the point I'd reached does things to you that a hangover can't touch."

I said, "Well, at last there's definite proof of murder, anyway. Do you think the trap was set for Otto Schley, or could it have been for someone else? Is he the only one who would normally have gone to the garage?"

Charlie nodded. "Yes. He always makes a round of the buildings before he turns in. Nobody else would be likely to, at night."

"You know everybody around here pretty well," I said. "Tell me something about— Well, about Lecky."

"Brilliant astronomer, but rather narrow-minded and intolerant."

"That's bad for Paul Bailey," I said. "I mean, now that the cat's out of the bag about his affair with Elsie. You think Lecky will fire him?"

"Oh, no. Lecky will overlook that. He doesn't expect his assistants to be saints. I meant that he's intolerant of people who disagree with him on astronomical matters. Tell him you think there isn't sufficient proof of the period-luminosity law for Cepheid variables—and you'd better duck. And he's touchy as hell about personal remarks. Very little sense of humor."

"He and Fillmore get along all right?"

"Fairly well. Fillmore's a solar system man, and Lecky doesn't know there's anything closer than a parsec away. They ignore each other's work. Fillmore's always grousing because he doesn't get much time with the scope."

I strolled over to the parapet and leaned my elbows on it, looking down into the shadow of the building on the ground below. Somewhere down there, eleven rattlesnakes were at large. Eleven? Or was it ten? Had the murderer brought the silent one, the de-rattled one, into the building with him?

And if so, for whom?

"For you, maybe," said Charlie.

Startled, I turned to look at him.

He was grinning. "Simple, my dear Wunderly—as my friend Darius Hill would say. I could almost hear you taking a mental census of rattlesnakes when you looked down there. And the next thing you'd wonder about was obvious. No, I haven't a detective complex like Darius has. How do you like Darius, by the way?"

"He could be taken in too large doses," I admitted. "Charlie, what do you know about Eric Andressen?"

"Not much. He's rather a puzzle. Smart all right but I think he missed his bent. He should have been an artist or a musician instead of a scientist. Just the opposite of Paul Bailey."

"Is Bailey good?"

"Good? He's a wiz in his field. He can think circles around the other assistants—even your Annabel."

"What's Bailey's specialty?"

"He's going to be an astrochemist. After university, he worked five years as research man in a commercial chem lab before he got into astronomy. I guess it was Zoe and her father who got him interested in chemistry on the cosmic scale. He knew Zoe at university. They were engaged."

I whistled. "Then this Elsie business must have hit Zoe pretty hard, didn't it?"

"Not at all. Bailey came here about eight months ago, and his engagement with Zoe lasted only a month after he came. And it was mutual; they just decided they'd made a mistake. And I guess they had at that. Their temperaments weren't suited to one another at all."

"And they're still on friendly terms?"

"Completely. What animosity there is seems to be between Bailey and Fillmore, instead of between Bailey and Zoe. Fillmore didn't like their decision to break the engagement and he seemed to blame Paul for it, although I'm pretty sure the original decision was Zoe's. They're still cool toward one another — Paul and Fillmore, I mean. But for other reasons."

"What kind of reasons?" I asked.

"Well — professional ones, in a way. I don't know the whole story but Fillmore was very friendly toward Paul when Paul and Zoe were engaged. He is really the one who persuaded Paul to come here as an assistant. And talked the board of regents, back in Los Angeles, into hiring Paul.

"Then he had a reaction when the engagement was broken. I think he tried to undermine Paul then and to get him fired. At any rate, he threatened to do it."

"Hmm," I said. "Sounds as though Fillmore isn't quite the disinterested scientist at heart."

"There may be something on his side," said Charlie. "Fillmore himself isn't too popular with Lecky and with the regents. And he thinks, rightly or wrongly, that Paul Bailey is shooting for his,

Fillmore's, job. If so, it's quite possible Paul will succeed. He's got an ingratiating personality and he knows how to rub Lecky the right way."

"Who has the say-so on hiring and firing—the director or the regents?"

"The regents, really. But under ordinary circumstances, they'd take Lecky's advice."

I glanced at the luminous dial of my wrist watch. "Getting late," I said. "If you're going to hunt those rattlesnakes at dawn, hadn't you better get some sleep?"

"Don't think I'll sleep tonight. It's too late, now, to turn in. And anyway— Oh, hell, I just don't want to sleep. I'm too jittery."

Design for Dying

Back in my room, I picked up the manuscript of the book Hill had given me. I was beginning to get a bit sleepy and "The Murderer's Guide" ought to affect that, one way or the other. I didn't care which way. If it made me sleepy, I'd sleep.

It started out slowly, dully. I was surprised, because the random paragraphs I had read previously had been far from dull. In fact, they'd been uneasy reading in a place where murder had just been done.

But, before I became really sleepy, I reached the second chapter. It was entitled "The Thrill of Killing; a Study in Atavism."

And here Darius really started to ride his hobby and to become eloquent about it. Man, he said, survived his early and precarious days by being a specialist in the art of killing. He killed to live, to eat, to obtain clothing in the form of furs. Killing was a necessary and natural function.

"Man," Darius wrote, *"has a gruesomely long heritage of murder. Nationalities, government, and progress are based upon it. The first inventions that raised man above the lesser beasts who were stronger than he, were means of murder—the club, the spear, the missile. . . .*

"Is it any wonder, then, that in most of us survives an atavistic tendency to kill? In many it is rationalized as a desire to indulge in the murder-sports of hunting and fishing.

"But occasionally this atavistic impulse breaks through to the surface in its original, primitive violence. Often the first step is an unintended slaying. The murderer, without really intending to do so, or forced to do so by circumstances beyond his control, has tasted blood. And blood, to a creature with man's heritage, can be more heady than wine. . . ."

And his third chapter was "The Mass Murderer; Artist of Crime."

A clever man who kills many, Hill wrote, is less likely to be caught and punished than one who commits a single crime. He gave a host of instances—uncaught and unpunished Jack-the-Rippers.

A single crime, he said, is almost always a strongly motivated one, and motivation gives it away. If a killer kills only for deep-lying cause, the motive can almost invariably be traced back to him and proved. On the contrary, a man who kills for the most casual and light of reasons is far less likely to be suspected of his crimes.

"The indigent heir who kills for a fortune, the betrayed husband who slays, the victim who kills his blackmailer—all these act from the most obvious of motives and are therefore doomed from the start, no matter how subtle the actual methods they use. The man who puts nicotine in another man's coffee merely because the latter is a bore, is far more likely to remain free.

"Taking advantage of this, the clever killer will often extend his crime from a single one to a series, one or more of which are, by design, completely without motive. Confronted with such a series, the police are helpless to use their usual effective methods."

There was more, much more, in this vein. Case after case quoted, most of them solved, if at all, only by a voluntary confession years after the crimes. Case after case of *series* of crimes which have never been solved to this day.

And suddenly, as I read something came to my mind with a shock.

Undoubtedly the murderer, the man or woman who had killed Elsie Willis and Otto Schley had read this very book. Was using it, in fact, as a blueprint for murder. . . .

There was a soft rap on my door. I said "Come in," and Charlie Lightfoot stuck his head in the doorway.

He said, "Come on down to the kitchen for coffee, Bill."

"Huh? At this time of night?"

Charlie grinned. "Night is day in an observatory, Bill. These guys never go to bed till later than this in seeing weather. Even in bad weather they stay up late out of habit. They always have coffee around this time."

Coffee sounded good, now that Hill's book had made me wakeful again. I said, "Sure, I'll be down in a minute," and Charlie went on.

I put on slippers instead of replacing my shoes, and put the manuscript away in a drawer of the bureau.

As I neared the bottom of the staircase, I noticed Fergus Fillmore writing at a desk in a niche off the hallway. I wondered for a moment why he didn't find it more convenient to work in his room—then I remembered he didn't have a room here, and was cut off from his own house until Charlie gathered in the rest of the rattlesnakes in the morning.

He looked up at me and nodded a greeting. "Hullo, Wunderly. I see you're turning nocturnal like the rest of us."

"Having coffee?" I asked him.

"In a few minutes. The police will be here tomorrow or the next day; they'll get through somehow. They'll want our testimony, and I'm making notes while things are fresh in my mind. I'm almost through."

"Good idea," I said. "I'll do the same when I get back upstairs."

I went on into the kitchen.

"It's cafeteria, Wunderly," Darius Hill told me. "Pour yourself a cup and sit down."

He, Charlie Lightfoot, Eric Andressen and Rex Parker were seated around the square table in the center of the big kitchen. Charlie slid his chair to make room for me. He said, "I guess Paul Bailey's asleep. I rapped lightly on his door and he didn't answer."

Andressen said, "He should sleep through all right; we gave him a pretty strong dose. Where's Fergus?"

"Right here," said Fillmore from the doorway. "Darius, what's this about your twisting the tails of spectroscopic binaries?"

"Haven't made them holler yet," said Darius slowly, "but maybe I've got something. Look, Fergus, on an eclipsing binary the maximum separation of the spectral lines when they are double determines the relative velocity of the stars in their orbits."

"Obviously."

"Therefore—" said Darius, and went on with it. At the fourth cosine, I quit listening and reached for a ham sandwich.

As I ate, I looked at the faces of the men around me. Charlie Lightfoot, Eric Andressen, Rex Parker, Fergus Fillmore, Darius Hill. . . . Was one of these men, I wondered, a murderer? Was one of these men even now planning further murders?

It seemed impossible, as I studied their faces. The Indian's haggard and worried, Hill and Fillmore eager on their abstruse discussion with Andressen listening intently and Rex looking bored.

Charlie was the first to leave, then Parker and Andressen together. When I stood up, Darius Hill stood also. He asked:

"Play chess, Wunderly?"

"A little," I admitted.

"Let's play a game before we turn in."

When we reached his room, he produced a beautiful set of ivory chessmen. He said apologetically, "Don't judge my game

HANDBOOK FOR HOMICIDE 89

by these men, Wunderly. They were given to me. I'm just a dub."

He wasn't, by a long shot. But I managed to hold him to a close game that resolved itself finally into a draw when I traded my last piece for his final pawn.

"Good game," he said. "Another?"

But I excused myself and left.

My slippers made no sound along the carpeted hallway. Possibly if I'd been noisy I'd have never seen that crack of faint light under the edge of Paul Bailey's door. Maybe it would have been turned off, in time.

But I saw it and stood there outside the door wondering whether it meant anything. If Bailey had awakened and turned on a lamp, certainly I'd make a fool of myself turning in an alarm.

Death Before Dawn

Yet if an intruder—the murderer—was in there, I'd warn him if I knocked on the door. There seemed only one way of finding out. I stooped down and looked into the keyhole.

All I could see was the desk at the far side of the room. The lamp on the desk wasn't on and the light that shone on the desk came from the right and couldn't be from the overhead bulb.

A flashlight? Someone standing still on the right side of the room, holding a flashlight pointing at the desk. But why would anyone be standing there?

Something else caught my eye; there was a lot of chemical equipment shoved back under the desk itself. Bottles, a rack of test tubes, a retort—and a DeWar flask.

I'm no chemist, but I do know what a DeWar flask is. And the moment I saw it, I knew how Elsie Willis had been killed. Knew, rather, why we had heard the sound of her fall downstairs *when* we heard it, just after Paul Bailey had walked into the living room.

As I straightened up from the keyhole I lost my balance.

Instinctively my hand grasped the doorknob to regain my equilibrium. And the doorknob rattled!

That ended the advantage of secrecy, and I hurled myself through the doorway.

The flashlight was there, but it was not being held. It was lying flat on the bureau.

There was no one in sight. The killer, then, was *behind* me on the same side of the room as the bed! I tried to turn around — too late. I didn't even feel the blow that felled me. . . .

Charlie Lightfoot was bending over me, and past him I could see a blur of other faces. Then my eyes came more nearly to focus and I could make out Annabel among them.

Charlie was saying, "Bill, are you all right?"

I sat up and put my hand back of my head. It hurt like hell. I took my hand away again.

"Bill!" It was Annabel's voice this time. "Are you all right?"

"I — I guess so," I said. And then, quite unnecessarily, "Somebody conked me. I —"

"You don't know who it was, Wunderly?" It was Darius Hill's voice.

I started to shake my head, but that hurt, so I answered verbally instead. Then, because I was beginning to wonder how long I'd been out, I asked Darius:

"How — how long has it been since I left your room?"

"About half an hour. Did this happen right after that?"

"Yes, only a minute or two after. I saw a light under Bailey's door. I busted in and turned the wrong way."

I tried to stand up. Charlie gave me a hand on one side and Annabel on the other. I made it, all right, but leaned back against the wall for a moment until I got over the slight dizziness.

Other people were talking excitedly and I had time to take inventory. Eric Andressen and Fergus Fillmore were both still fully dressed. Darius had a lounging robe and slippers on but still wore trousers and shirt under the robe. Paul Bailey, looking sleepy and as though he was suffering from a bad hangover, was sitting on the edge of the bed, a bathrobe thrown across his shoulders over pajamas. Annabel wore a dressing gown.

Charlie Lightfoot and Rex Parker, who was standing in the doorway, were both fully dressed.

I said, "Charlie, who found me?"

"I did, on my way down from the roof. You groaned as I was going by the door. I thought it was Paul groaning but I came in."

Fillmore asked, "What was the yell that brought us all running? I heard it downstairs."

Charlie grunted. "That was Paul. He must've been having a nightmare. When I shook him he let out a yowl like a steam engine before he woke up."

Bailey said, "I thought—

"Hell, I don't know *what* I thought. I don't remember yelling—but if Charlie says I did, I guess I did."

"Lecky," said Darius Hill. "We'll have to let Lecky know."

"He can't get over here before dawn," Fillmore pointed out, "unless he wants to run the gauntlet of rattlesnakes. We'd just wake him up."

Charlie said, "Darius is right. Something else has happened. We ought to let Lecky know. What time is it?"

"Four-thirty," Hill said.

"Then it'll be light in less than an hour. I'll go find those other snakes. But if I don't find them all right away, I'll escort Lecky over here—beat trail for him. I can take Fergus too, if he wants to get back home."

Darius Hill had walked over to the window and looked out. "There's a light over at Lecky's house. I'm going to phone now. Let's all go downstairs to the living room."

We went down in more or less of a group, Darius going ahead. He went into the room where the house telephone was, and the rest of us herded into the living room. All of us were quiet and subdued; none seemed able or willing to offer much comment on the situation we were in.

Darius would probably have been verbose enough, if he'd been there, but Darius wasn't there. He was taking an unconscionably long time at the telephone. For some reason, it worried me.

I strolled to the door of the hall without attracting attention and went down the hall and into the room which Darius had entered.

He was at the phone, listening, and I could see from the whiteness of his face that something was wrong.

". . . .Yes, Mrs. Lecky," he said. Then a long pause. "You're *sure* you don't want one of us to come over right away? I know it's almost dawn but —"

He talked a minute longer, then put down the phone and looked at me.

He said, slowly, "Lecky's dead, Wunderly. Good old Lecky. She found him at his desk just now with a knife in his back."

Then suddenly the words were tumbling out of him so fast that they were hardly coherent. "Good Lord! I thought I knew something about criminology and detection. What a damn fool I was! This is my fault, Wunderly, for pretending to be so damn smart about something.

"My fault. That book. I don't know who's doing these murders — I can't even guess — but he got the idea out of that damned book of mine. Just to be clever, I started something that —"

I said, "But it isn't your fault, Hill. What you wrote in that book is true, in a way."

"I'm going to burn that manuscript, Wunderly. What business has a fat old fool like me to give advice that — that gets people killed? Somebody's committing murder by the book — and the worst of it is that *the book's right.* That's why I should never have written it. . . ."

HANDBOOK FOR HOMICIDE 93

There wasn't any use arguing with him.

"When was Lecky killed?" I asked.

"Just now. Less than fifteen minutes ago. While you were unconscious upstairs, probably."

"The hell," I said. "How do you know it was *then?* You said his wife just found him."

"She was talking to him fifteen minutes before. He was in his study typing. She'd been in bed but waked up. She told him to come on to bed and he answered.

"Then just now—fifteen minutes after that—she heard the phone ring . . . my call. And it wasn't answered, so she came downstairs and—found him dead."

"Lord," I said, "and she had wits enough to answer the phone right away and give you the details without getting hysterical?"

"You haven't met Mrs. Lecky, or you'd understand. Damn! One of us ought to go over there, though. It's almost light enough. Charlie could put his leggings on and—"

"Wait!" I said. "I've got—"

I thought it over a second and the more I thought about it the better it looked. It might work.

"Darius," I said, "look, if whoever killed Lecky is among the group in the living room—and it *must* be one of them—then he just got back into this building five or ten minutes ago."

"Of course. But how—?"

"Murderers aren't any braver than anyone else. He wouldn't have crossed an area where there were rattlesnakes loose without taking precautions. See what I mean? Whoever went over there and back would have put on puttees or leggings under his trousers."

"I—I suppose he would. And—you think he wouldn't have had a chance to take them off again?"

"I doubt it," I told him. "He must have been just getting into the building when Paul Bailey let out that yell. And everybody converged on Bailey's room. He'd have to go along to avoid suspicion; he'd be the last one to want to give himself away by being late getting there!

"And since then, he certainly hasn't had a chance to be alone."

Darius' eyes gleamed. He said, "Wunderly, it's a chance! A good chance."

He grabbed my arm, but I held back.

"Wait," I said, "this has got to be your idea—not mine."

"Why?"

"Your position here, your seniority. Your work. Look some people may figure as you did just now—blame that book of yours for a share of what happened. But if *you* solve the murders, you'll be exonerated. The credit for that idea doesn't mean anything to me. I'd rather you took it."

He stared at me hopefully but almost unbelievingly. "You mean, knowing I'm a bag of wind, you'd—"

"You're not," I said. "You're one of the best astronomers living. And it was that phobia of yours—not your fault—that led you to write what you did. I agree you should never have it published. But in writing it—you stuck your neck out, as far as your colleagues are concerned. It means everything to you to solve the murders. It means nothing to me."

His hand gripped my upper arm and squeezed hard. "I—I don't know how to thank—"

"Don't try," I said. "Let's go."

We went into the other room and I walked over and stood beside Annabel while Hill announced the death of the director. He told them, quite simply, quite unemotionally, what had happened.

And then while they were still shocked by the news, he sprang the suggestion that each man in the group immediately prove he was not wearing protection of any sort on his lower legs.

"I'll lead off," he said.

He lifted the cuffs of his trousers up as high as the bottom of the lounging robe he was wearing over them, exposing neatly-clocked black socks.

Paul Bailey chuckled nervously. He had seated himself cross-legged in the morris chair, and his rather short pajama trousers were already twisted halfway up the calves of his bare legs. He said, "I believe I can join the white sheep without even moving."

The Last Battle

None of us quite knew what had happened, at first. The sound of a shot, unexpected in the confined space of a room, can be paralyzing as well as deafening.

We heard the thud of the falling body before any of us — unless it was Darius — knew who had been shot. For Darius was the only one who had been facing Fergus Fillmore, who had been standing at the back of the group in a corner of the room.

Charlie Lightfoot and I were the first ones to reach him. The revolver — a small pearl-handled one — was still in his right hand, and the shot had been fired with its muzzle pressed to his temple.

Charlie's gesture of feeling for the beat of Fillmore's heart was perfunctory. He said wonderingly, "I suppose this means that *he* — But in heaven's name, *why?*"

I nodded toward Fillmore's ankles, exposed where his fall had hiked up the cuffs of his trouser-legs above the tops of his high shoes. Under the trousers a pair of heavy leggings were laced on.

"Mine," said Charlie.

Hill said, "Isn't — isn't that the corner of an envelope sticking just past the lapel of his coat?"

Surprised, I looked up at Darius Hill. He was standing very rigidly, his hands clenched. But he was looking at the corpse; he had, to that extent at least, overcome his necrophobia.

Charlie took the envelope from Fillmore's inside coat pocket. It was addressed to Darius.

And Hill, his face pale and waxen, but his voice steady, read to us the letter it contained:

"Dear Darius: Are you really a criminologist, or are you a monumental bluff? I have a hunch it's hot air, my dear Darius, but if you ever read this letter, I apologize. It will mean that you were more clever that I—or perhaps I should say you are more clever than the book you wrote. To meet that contingency, I carry a pistol—for a purpose you have already discovered. It would be quite absurd for a man of my position to stand trial for murder. You will understand that.

"I am writing this at the desk in the hallway. As soon as I finish writing, I shall join you for coffee and a sandwich in the kitchen. Then I shall carry out the third step in the program which has been forced upon me by the necessity of keeping my neck out of a noose.

"I remembered your book, Darius, as soon as I discovered, early this evening, that Elsie was dead. She walked into Paul Bailey's room early this evening while I was searching that room to get back the letter which Paul had held as a threat over my head—"

Darius Hill looked up from the letter and said to Bailey, "What letter is that, Paul?"

The bewilderment on Bailey's face seemed genuine enough.

Then, suddenly, *"That* letter! Good grief, he thought I still had it. Why, I'd destroyed it months ago."

"What *was* it?"

"One Fergus wrote me about ten months ago, while he was trying to get me to take the job here. He talked too freely—or rather—wrote too freely, in that letter."

"What do you mean, Paul?" Darius demanded.

"He criticized Dr. Lecky—pretty viciously. And said some things Lecky would never have forgiven, if he'd ever seen the letter. And he took some swipes at the regents in Los Angeles, too. From what I've learned since about how touchy Lecky was, I have a hunch that letter would have cost Fillmore his job—if either Lecky or the regents had ever seen it. But I didn't keep it. I threw it away before I packed my stuff to come here."

"But you threatened Fillmore with it, later?"

Bailey shifted uneasily in his chair. "Well—not exactly, no. But when Zoe broke our engagement—and it *was* Zoe who broke it—Fillmore had the crust to tell me that unless I managed to patch things up between Zoe and me, he'd see that I lost my job. We had some words and I told him his own job wasn't any too secure if Lecky and the regents knew what he'd written about them. I didn't threaten him with the letter but he may have got the impression I still had it."

Darius turned back to the letter and resumed reading:

"I happened to be to the left of the door, and Elsie walked in without seeing me. But in a moment, I knew, she would turn. I acted involuntarily, although I swear my intention was merely to stun her so I could leave the room without being identified.

"I was standing beside the bureau and I picked up the first convenient object—a hairbrush. I struck with the back of it.

"Then I found—as I caught her and lowered her to the floor so there would be no sound of a fall—that I was a murderer. A man after your own heart, Darius.

"And it was then that I recalled those lessons in your book, about how to get away with murder. Recalled them after I was already, inadvertently, a murderer. And some of the things in your manuscript make sense, Darius. As you say, a killer of several suffers no worse penalty than a killer of one.

"I forced myself, very deliberately, to sit down for a few minutes and think out a course of action. First, an alibi. I could not prove I was elsewhere when Elsie was killed but I could make her seem to be killed when I was elsewhere—playing bridge.

"A DeWar flask was the answer to that. I went downstairs,

found Bailey and set him a task with the blink-mike which would keep him busy for an hour. Then I went to the lab and liquefied some air, taking it upstairs in the flask.

"Extreme cold applied to the leg joints of the body froze them, and I propped the corpse erect in a corner. By the time the flesh thawed and she fell, I was playing bridge downstairs with several of you. Was that not simple, Darius? Is this news to you, or had you solved the method?

"Even the coroner's examination of the body will not show what happened, because I'll see to it there is a leak in the tubing of the makeshift refrigerator we rigged up to preserve the body."

Rex Parker's voice cut in. "I'd better check that right away, Mr. Hill."

Hill nodded and read on, as Parker left the room. "But Otto Schley saw me leaving Bailey's room. It meant nothing to him then and he mentioned it to no one. But he will be a source of danger if the police ferret out—or you ferret out—the fact that Elsie's death did not occur during the bridge game but at about the time Otto saw me.

"So I remembered your book, Darius. And my method of dealing with Otto needs no explaining.

"A fortunate accident added to the confusion. I refer to the rattlesnake with the missing rattle—or the rattle from the missing rattlesnake. I had nothing to do with that. Wunderly says he slammed the door on a snake, and it is probable that the closing of the door knocked off or pinched off the rattle."

I said, "Damn," softly to myself.

"But now all is quiet again," Darius Hill continued reading. "Bailey is asleep under a mild drug. After coffee, I shall go to complete my search of his room. I am almost convinced, by now, that he does not have the letter any longer and that his tacit threat was a bluff.

"And then, whether or not I find it, a third and final murder.

"You see, Darius, I have taken your lessons to heart. No one will suspect that I would kill Lecky merely because—whether you or I receive the directorship—I shall be freer to concentrate on lunar and planetary observations and no longer will take orders from a doddering fool.

"No, I would *not* kill him if I had a stronger motive than that. I shall not kill Bailey, for that very reason. If I succeed to the directorship, however, he would be taken care of. Of course, I would not kill Lecky for so slight a motive, as motives go, save that the doing of two murders has made a third a matter of slight moment.

"Adieu, then, Darius. Coffee, then Bailey's room, then I shall steal Charlie Lightfoot's leather leggings from the closet, lace them on, and visit friend Lecky. Then—but if you ever read this, you'll know the rest."

Darius looked up. He said, in a curiously flat voice, "That's all."

* * * *

A month later, Annabel and I were married at the observatory. Darius Hill, the director, had insisted on giving the bride away. Charlie Lightfoot was my best man.

Darius spoke, copiously, at the dinner afterwards. He'd been at it for what seemed like hours.

". . . and it is most fitting that Einar should be the setting for this sacred ceremony," said Darius, "wherein are joined the most beautiful woman who ever graced a problem in differential calculus, and a young man who, although he came to us in an hour of tribulation, has proved. . . ."

"Ugh," said Charlie Lightfoot. "Paleface talk too much."

He reached for his glass—and I reached, under the table, for Annabel's hand.

BEFORE SHE KILLS

The door was that of an office in an old building on State Street near Chicago Avenue, on the near north side, and the lettering on it read HUNTER & HUNTER DETECTIVE AGENCY. I opened it and went in. Why not? I'm one of the Hunters; my name is Ed. The other Hunter is my uncle, Ambrose Hunter.

The door to the inner office was open and I could see Uncle Am playing solitaire at his desk in there. He's shortish, fattish and smartish, with a straggly brown mustache. I waved at him and headed for my desk in the outer office. I'd had my lunch — we take turns — and he'd be leaving now.

Except that he wasn't. He swept the cards together and stacked them but he said, "Come on in, Ed. Something to talk over with you."

I went in and pulled up a chair. It was a hot day and two big flies were droning in circles around the room. I reached for the fly swatter and held it, waiting for one or both of them to light somewhere. "We ought to get a bomb," I said.

"Huh? Who do we want to blow up?"

"A bug bomb," I said. "One of these aerosol deals, so we can get flies on the wing."

"Not sporting, kid. Like shooting a sitting duck, only the opposite. Got to give the flies a chance."

"All right," I said, swatting one of them as it landed on a corner of the desk. "What did you want to talk about?"

"A case, maybe. A client, or a potential one, came in while you were feeding your face. Offered us a job, but I'm not sure about taking it. Anyway, it's one you'd have to handle, and I wanted to talk it over with you first."

The other fly landed and died, and the wind of the swat that killed it blew a small rectangular paper off the desk onto the floor. I picked it up and saw that it was a check made out to Hunter & Hunter and signed Oliver R. Bookman—a name I didn't recognize. It was for five hundred dollars.

We could use it. Business had been slow for a month or so. I said, "Looks like you took the job already. Not that I blame you." I put the check back on the desk. "That's a pretty strong argument."

"No, I didn't take it. Ollie Bookman had the check already made out when he came, and put it down while we were talking. But I told him we weren't taking the case till I'd talked to you."

"Ollie? Do you know him, Uncle Am?"

"No, but he told me to call him that, and it comes natural. He's that kind of guy. Nice, I mean."

I took his word for it. My uncle is a nice guy himself, but he's a sharp judge of character and can spot a phony a mile off.

He said, "He thinks his wife is trying to kill him or maybe planning to."

"Interesting," I said. "But what could we do about it—unless she does? And then it's cop business."

"He knows that, but he's not sure enough to do anything drastic about it unless someone backs up his opinion and tells him he's not imagining things. Then he'll decide what to do. He wants you to study things from the inside."

"Like how? And why me?"

"He's got a young half brother living in Seattle whom his wife has never met and whom he hasn't seen for twenty years. Brother's twenty-five years old—and you can pass for that age. He wants you to come to Chicago from Seattle on business and stay with them for a few days. You wouldn't even have to change your first name; you'd be Ed Cartwright and Ollie would brief you on everything you'll be supposed to know."

I thought a moment and then said, "Sounds a little far out to me, but—" I glanced pointedly at the five-hundred-dollar check. "Did you ask how he happened to come to us?"

"Yes. Koslovsky sent him; he's a friend of Kossy's, belongs to a couple of the same clubs." Koslovsky is chief investigator for an insurance company; we've worked for him or with him on several things.

I asked, "Does that mean there's an insurance angle?"

"No, Ollie Bookman carries only a small policy—small relative to what his estate would be—that he took out a long time ago. Currently he's not insurable. Heart trouble."

"Oh. And does Kossy approve this scheme of his for investigating his wife?"

"I was going to suggest we ask Kossy that. Look, Ed, Ollie's coming back for our answer at two o'clock. I'll have time to eat and get back. But I wanted to brief you before I left so you could think it over. You might also call Koslovsky and get a rundown on Ollie, whatever he knows about him."

Uncle Am got up and got the old black slouch hat he insists on wearing despite the season. Kidding him about it does no good.

I said, "One more question before you go. Suppose Bookman's wife meets his half brother, his real one, someday. Isn't it going to be embarrassing?"

"I asked him that. He says it's damned unlikely; he and his

brother aren't at all close. He'll never go to Seattle and the chances that his brother will ever come to Chicago are one in a thousand. Well, so long, kid."

I called Koslovsky. Yes, he'd recommended us to Bookman when Bookman had told him what he wanted done and asked — knowing that he, Koslovsky, sometimes hired outside investigators when he and his small staff had a temporary overload of cases — to have an agency recommended to him.

"I don't think too much of his idea," Koslovsky said, "but, hell, it's his money and he can afford it. If he wants to spend some of it that way, you might as well have the job as anyone else."

"Do you think there's any real chance that he's right? About his wife, I mean."

"I wouldn't know, Ed. I've met her a time or two and — well, she struck me as a cold potato, probably, but hardly as a murderess. Still, I don't know her well enough to say."

"How well do you know Bookman? Well enough to know whether he's pretty sane or gets wild ideas?"

"Always struck me as pretty sane. We're not close friends but I've known him fairly well for three or four years."

"Just how well off is he?"

"Not rich, but solvent. If I had to guess, I'd say he could cash out at over one hundred thousand, less than two. Enough to kill him for, I guess."

"What's his racket?"

"Construction business, but he's mostly retired. Not on account of age; he's only in his forties. But he's got angina pectoris, and a year or two ago the medicos told him to take it easy or else."

Uncle Am got back a few minutes before two o'clock and I just had time to tell him about my conversation with Kossy before Ollie Bookman showed up. Bookman was a big man with a round, cheerful face that made you like him at sight. He had a good handshake.

"Hi, Ed," he said. "Glad that's your name because it's what I'll be calling you even if it wasn't. That is, if you'll take on the job for me. Your Uncle Am here wouldn't make it definite. What do you say?"

I told him we could at least talk about it and when we were comfortably seated in the inner office, I said, "Mr. Bookman—"
"Call me Ollie," he interrupted, so I said, "All right, Ollie. The only reason I can think of, thus far, for not taking on the job, if we don't, is that even if you're right—if your wife does have any thoughts about murder—the chances seem awfully slight that I could find out about it, and how she intended to do it, in time to stop it."

He nodded. "I understand that, but I want you to try, anyway. You see, Ed, I'll be honest and say that I *may* be imagining things. I want somebody else's opinion—after that somebody has lived with us at least a few days. But if you come to agree with me, or find any positive indications that I'm maybe right, then— well, I'll do something about it. Eve—that's my wife's name— won't give me a divorce or even agree to a separation with maintenance, but damn it, I can always simply leave home and live at the club—better that than get myself killed."

"You have asked her to give you a divorce, then?"

"Yes, I— Let me begin at the beginning. Some of this is going to be embarrassing to tell, but you should know the whole score. I met Eve . . ."

2

He'd met Eve eight years ago when he was thirty-five and she was twenty-five, or so she claimed. She was a strip-tease dancer who worked in night clubs under the professional name of Eve Eden—her real name had been Eve Packer. She was a statuesque blonde, beautiful. Ollie had fallen for her and started a campaign immediately, a campaign that intensified when he learned that offstage she was quiet, modest, the exact opposite of what strippers are supposed to be and which some of them really are. By the time he was finally having an affair with her, lust had ripened into respect and he'd been thinking in any case that it was about time he married and settled down.

So he married her, and that was his big mistake. She turned out to be completely, psychopathically frigid. She'd been acting, and doing a good job of acting, during the weeks before marriage, but after marriage, or at least after the honeymoon, she simply saw no reason to keep on acting. She had what she wanted — security and respectability. She hated sex, and that was that. She turned Ollie down flat when he tried to get her to go to a psychoanalyst or even to a marriage consultant, who, he thought, might be able to talk her into going to an analyst. In every other way she was a perfect wife. Beautiful enough to be a showpiece that made all his friends envy him, a charming hostess, even good at handling servants and running the house. For all outsiders could know, it was a perfect marriage. But for a while it drove Ollie Bookman nuts. He offered to let her divorce him and make a generous settlement, either lump sum or alimony. But she had what she wanted, marriage and respectability, and she wasn't going to give them up and become a divorcee, even if doing so wasn't going to affect her scale of living in the slightest. He threatened to divorce her, and she laughed at him. He had, she pointed out, no grounds for divorce that he could prove in court, and she'd never give him any. She'd simply deny the only thing he could say about her, and make a monkey out of him.

It was an impossible situation, especially as Ollie had badly wanted to have children or at least a child, as well as a normal married life. He'd made the best of it by accepting the situation at home as irreparable and settling for staying sane by making at least occasional passes in other directions. Nothing serious, just a normal man wanting to live a normal life and succeeding to a degree.

BEFORE SHE KILLS 107

But eventually the inevitable happened. Three years ago, he had found himself in an affair that turned out to be much more than an affair, the real love of his life—and a reciprocated love. She was a widow, Dorothy Stark, in her early thirties. Her husband had died five years before in Korea; they'd had only a honeymoon together before he'd gone overseas. Ollie wanted so badly to marry her that he offered Eve a financial settlement that would have left him relatively a pauper—this was before the onset of his heart trouble and necessary semiretirement; he looked forward to another twenty years or so of earning capacity—but she refused; never would she consent to become a divorcee, at any price. About this time, he spent a great deal of money on private detectives in the slim hope that her frigidity was toward him only, but the money was wasted. She went out quite a bit but always to bridge parties, teas or, alone or with respectable woman companions, to movies or plays.

Uncle Am interrupted. "You said you used private detectives before, Ollie. Out of curiosity, can I ask why you're not using the same outfit again?"

"Turned out to be crooks, Am. When they and I were finally convinced we couldn't get anything on her legitimately, they offered for a price to frame her for me." He mentioned the name of an agency we'd heard of, and Uncle Am nodded.

Ollie went on with his story. There wasn't much more of it. Dorothy Stark had known that he could never marry her but she also knew that he very badly wanted a child, preferably a son, and had loved him enough to offer to bear one for him. He had agreed—even if he couldn't give the child his name, he wanted one—and two years ago she had borne him a son: Jerry, they'd named him, Jerry Stark. Ollie loved the boy to distraction.

Uncle Am asked if Eve Bookman knew of Jerry's existence and Ollie nodded.

"But she won't do anything about it. What could she do, except divorce me?"

"But if that's the situation," I asked him, "what motive would your wife have to want to kill you? And why now, if the situation has been the same for two years?"

"There's been one change, Ed, very recently. Two years ago, I made out a new will, without telling Eve. You see, with angina pectoris, my doctor tells me it's doubtful if I have more than a few years to live in any case. And I want at least the bulk of my estate to go to Dorothy and to my son. So— Well, I made out a will which leaves a fourth to Eve, a fourth to Dorothy and half, in trust, to Jerry. And I explained, in a preamble, why I was doing it that way—the true story of my marriage to Eve and the fact that it really wasn't one, and why it wasn't. And I admitted paternity of Jerry. You see, Eve could contest that will—but would she? If she fought it, the newspapers would have a field day with its contents and make a big scandal out of it—and her position, her respectability, is the most important thing in the world to Eve. Of course, it would hurt Dorothy, too—but if she won, even in part, she could always move somewhere else and change her name. Jerry, if this happens in the next few years as it probably will, will be too young to be hurt, or even to know what's going on. You see?"

"Yes," I said. "But if you hate your wife, why not—"

"Why not simply disinherit her completely, leave her nothing? Because then she *would* fight the will, she'd have to. I'm hoping by giving her a fourth, she'll decide she'd rather settle for that and save face than contest the will."

"I see that," I said. "But the situation's been the same for two years now. And you said that something recent—"

"As recent as last night," he interrupted. "I kept that will in a hiding place in my office—which is in my home since I retired— and last night I discovered it was missing. It was there a few days ago. Which means that, however she came to do so, Eve found it. And destroyed it. So if I should die now—she thinks—before

BEFORE SHE KILLS

I discover the will is gone and make another, I'll die intestate and she'll automatically get everything. She's got well over a hundred thousand dollars' worth of motive for killing me before I find out the will is gone."

Uncle Am asked, "You say 'she thinks.' Wouldn't she?"

"Last night she would have," Ollie said grimly. "But this morning, I went to my lawyer, made out a new will, same provisions, and left it in his hands. Which is what I should have done with the first one. But she doesn't know that, and I don't want her to."

It was my turn to question that. "Why not?" I wanted to know. "If she knows a new will exists, where she can't get at it, she'd know killing you wouldn't accomplish anything for her. Even if she got away with it."

"Right, Ed. But I'm almost hoping she will try, and fail. Then I'd be the happiest man on earth. I *would* have grounds for divorce—attempted murder should be grounds if anything is—and I could marry Dorothy, legitimize my son and leave him with my name. I—well, for the chance of doing that, I'm willing to take the chance of Eve's trying and succeeding. I haven't got much to lose, and everything to gain. How otherwise could I ever marry Dorothy—unless Eve should predecease me, which is damned unlikely. She's healthy as a horse, and younger than I am, besides. And if she should succeed in killing me, but got caught, she'd inherit nothing; Dorothy and Jerry would get it all. That's the law, isn't it? That no one can inherit from someone he's killed, I mean. Well, that's the whole story. Will you take the job, Ed, or do I have to look for someone else? I hope I won't."

I looked at Uncle Am—we never decide anything important without consulting one another—and he said, "Okay by me, kid." So I nodded to Ollie. "All right," I said.

3

We worked out details. He'd already checked plane flights and knew that a Pacific Airlines plane was due in from Seattle at ten fifteen that evening; I'd arrive on that and meanwhile he'd pretend to have received a telegram saying I was coming and would be in Chicago for a few days to a week on business, and asking him to meet the plane if convenient. I went him one better on that by telling him we knew a girl who sometimes did part-time work for us as a female operative and I'd have her phone his place, pretend to be a Western Union operator, and read the telegram to whoever answered the phone. He thought that was a good idea, especially if his wife was the one to take it down. We worked out the telegram itself and then he phoned his place on the pretext of wanting to know if his wife would be there to accept a C.O.D. package. She was, so I phoned the girl I had in mind, had her take down the telegram, and gave her Ollie's number to phone it to. We had the telegram dated from Denver, since the real Ed, if he were to get in that evening, would already be on the plane and would have to send the telegram from a stop en route. I told Ollie I'd work out a plausible explanation as to why I hadn't decided, until en route, to ask him to meet the plane.

Actually, we arranged to meet downtown, in the lobby of the Morrison Hotel an hour before plane time; Ollie lived north and if he were really driving to the airport, it would take him another hour to get there and an hour back as far as the Loop, so we'd have two hours to kill in further planning and briefing. Besides another half hour or so driving to his place when it was time to head there.

That meant he wouldn't have to brief me on family history now; there'd be plenty of time this evening. I did ask what kind of work Ed Cartwright did, so if necessary I could spend the rest of the afternoon picking up at least the vocabulary of whatever kind of work it was. But it turned out he ran a printing shop—

BEFORE SHE KILLS

which was a lucky break since after high school and before getting with my Uncle Am, I'd spent a couple of years as an apprentice printer myself and knew enough about the trade to talk about it casually.

Just as Ollie was getting ready to leave, the phone rang and it was our girl calling back to say she'd read the telegram to a woman who'd answered the phone and identified herself as Mrs. Oliver Bookman, so we were able to tell Ollie the first step had been taken.

After Ollie had left, Uncle Am looked at me and asked, "What do you think, kid?"

"I don't know," I said. "Except that five hundred bucks is five hundred bucks. Shall I mail the check in for deposit now, since I won't be here tomorrow?"

"Okay. Go out and mail it if you want and take the rest of the day off, since you'll start working tonight."

"All right. With this check in hand, I'm going to pick me up a few things, like a couple shirts and some socks. And how about a good dinner tonight? I'll meet you at Ireland's at six."

He nodded, and I went to my desk in the outer office and was making out a deposit slip and an envelope when he came and sat on the corner of the desk.

"Kid," he said. "This Ollie just *might* be right. We got to assume that he could be, anyway. And I just had a thought. What would be the safest way to kill a man with bad heart trouble, like angina pectoris is? I'd say conning him into having an attack by giving him a shock or by getting him to overexert himself somehow. Or else by substituting sugar pills for whatever he takes—nitroglycerin pills, I think it is—when he gets an attack."

I said, "I've been thinking along those lines myself, Uncle Am. I thought maybe one thing I'd do down in the Loop is have a talk with Doc Kruger." Kruger is our family doctor, sort of. He doesn't get much business from either of us but we use him for an information booth whenever we want to know something about forensic medicine.

"Wait a second," Uncle Am said. "I'll phone him. Maybe he'll let us buy him dinner with us tonight to pay him for picking his brains."

He went in the office and used his phone; I heard him talking to Doc. He came out and said, "It's a deal. Only at seven instead of six. That'll be better for you, anyway, Ed. Bring your suitcase with you and if we take our time at Ireland's, you can go right from there to meet Ollie and not have to go home again."

So I did my errands, went to our room, cleaned up and dressed, and packed a suitcase. I didn't think anybody would be looking in it to check up on me, but I thought I might as well be as careful as I could. I couldn't provide clothes with Seattle labels but I could and did avoid things with labels that said Chicago or were from well-known Chicago stores. And I avoided anything that was monogrammed, not that I particularly like monograms or have many things with them. Then I doodled around with my trombone until it was time to head for Ireland's.

I got there exactly on time and Doc and Uncle Am were there already. But there were three Martinis on the table; Uncle Am had known I wouldn't be more than a few minutes late, if any, so he'd ordered for me.

Without having to be asked, since Uncle Am had mentioned it over the phone, Doc started telling us about angina pectoris. It was incurable, he said, but a victim of it might live a long time if he took good care of himself. He had to avoid physical exertion like lifting anything heavy or climbing stairs. He had to avoid overtiring himself by doing even light work for a long period. He had to avoid overindulgence in alcohol, although an occasional drink wouldn't hurt him if he was in good physical shape otherwise. He had to avoid violent emotional upsets as far as was possible, and a fit of anger could be as dangerous as running up a flight of stairs.

Yes, nitroglycerin pills were used. Everyone suffering from angina carried them and popped one or two into his mouth any time he felt an attack coming on. They either prevented the attack or made it much lighter than it would have been otherwise. Doc took a little pillbox out of his pocket and showed us some nitro pills. They were white and very tiny.

There was another drug also used to avert or limit attacks that was even more effective than nitroglycerin. It was amyl nitrite and came in glass ampoules. In emergency, you crushed the ampoule and inhaled the contents. But amyl nitrite, Doc told us, was used less frequently than nitroglycerin, and only in very bad cases or for attacks in which nitro didn't seem to be helping, because repeated use of amyl nitrite diminished the effect; the victim built up immunity to it if he used it often.

Doc had really come loaded. He'd brought an amyl nitrite ampoule with him, too, and showed it to us. I asked him if I could have it, just in case. He gave it to me without asking why, and even showed me the best way to hold it and crush it if I ever had to use it.

We had a second cocktail and I asked him a few more questions and got answers to them, and that pretty well covered angina pectoris, and then we ordered. Ireland's is famous for sea food; it's probably the best inland sea-food restaurant in the country, and we all ordered it. Doc Kruger and Uncle Am wrestled with lobsters; me, I'm a coward — I ate royal sole.

4

Doc had to take off after our coffee, but it was still fifteen or twenty minutes too early for me to leave — I'd have to take a taxi to the Morrison on account of having a suitcase; otherwise, I'd have walked and been just right on the timing — so Uncle Am and I had a second coffee apiece and yakked. He said he felt like taking a walk before he turned in, so he'd ride in the taxi with me and then walk home from there.

I fought off a bellboy who tried to take my suitcase away from me and made myself comfortable on one of the overstuffed chairs in the lobby. I'd sat there about five or ten minutes when I heard myself being paged. I stood up and waved to the bellboy who'd been doing the paging and he came over and told me I was wanted on the phone and led me to the phone I was wanted on. I bought him off for four bits and answered the phone. It was Ollie Bookman, as I'd known it would be. Only he and Uncle Am would have known I was here and Uncle Am had left me only ten minutes ago.

"Ed," he said. "Change of plans. Eve wasn't doing anything this evening and decided to come to the airport with me, for the ride. I couldn't tell her no, for no reason. So you'll have to grab a cab and get out there ahead of us."

"Okay," I said. "Where are you now?"

"On the way south, at Division Street. Made an excuse to stop in a drugstore; didn't know how to get in touch with you until the time of our appointment. You can make it ahead of us if you get a cabby to hurry. I'll stall—drive as slow as I can without making Eve wonder. And I can stop for gas, and have my tires checked."

"What do I do at the airport if the plane's late?"

"Don't worry about the plane. You take up a spot near the Pacific Airlines counter; you'll see me come toward it and intercept me. Won't matter if the plane's in yet or not. I'll get us the hell out of there fast before Eve can learn if the plane's in. I'll make sure not to get there *before* arrival time."

"Right," I said. "But, Ollie, I'm not supposed to have seen you for twenty years—and I was five then, or supposed to be. So how would I recognize you? Or, for that matter, you recognize me?"

"No sweat, Ed. We write each other once a year, at Christmas. And several times, including last Christmas, we traded snapshots with our Christmas letters. Remember?"

BEFORE SHE KILLS

"Of course," I said. "But didn't your wife see the one I sent you?"

"She may have glanced at it casually. But after seven months she wouldn't remember it. Besides, you and the real Ed Cartwright are about the same physical type, anyway—dark hair, good looking. You'll pass. But don't miss meeting us before we reach the counter or somebody there might tell us the plane's not in yet, if it's not. Well, I better not talk any longer."

I swore a little to myself as I left the Morrison lobby and went to the cab rank. I'd counted on the time Ollie and I would have had together to have him finish my briefing. This way I'd have to let him do most of the talking, at least tonight. Well, he seemed smart enough to handle it. I didn't even know my parents' names, whether either of them was alive, whether I had any other living relatives besides Ollie. I didn't even know whether I was married or not—although I felt reasonably sure Ollie would have mentioned it if I was.

Yes, he'd have to do most of the talking—although I'd better figure out what kind of business I'd come to Chicago to do; I'd be supposed to know that, and Ollie wouldn't know anything about it. Well, I'd figure that out on the cab ride.

Barring accidents, I'd get there well ahead of Ollie, and I didn't want accidents, so I didn't offer the cabby any bribe for speed when I told him to take me to the airport. He'd keep the meter ticking all right, since he made his money by the mile and not by the minute.

I had my cover story ready by the time we got there. It wasn't detailed, but I didn't anticipate being pressed for details, and if I was, I knew more about printing equipment than Eve Bookman would know. I was a good ten minutes ahead of plane time. I found myself a seat near the Pacific Airlines counter and facing in the direction from which the Bookmans would come. Fifteen minutes later—on time, as planes go—the public-address system announced the arrival of my flight from Seattle, and fifteen minutes after that — time for me to have left the plane and even to have collected the suitcase that was by my feet — I saw them coming. That is, I saw Ollie coming, and with him was a beautiful, *soignée* blonde who could only be Eve Bookman, nee Eve Eden. Quite a dish. She was, with high heels, just about two inches short of Ollie's height, which made her just about as tall as I, unless she took off her shoes for me. Which, from what Ollie had told me about her, was about the last thing I expected her to do, especially here in the airport.

I got up and walked toward them and — remembering identification was only from snapshot — didn't put too much confidence in my voice when I asked, "Ollie?" and I put out my hand but only tentatively.

Ollie grabbed my hand in his big one and started pumping it. "Ed! Gawdamn if I can believe it, after all these years. When I last saw you, not counting pictures, you looked— Hell, let's get to that later. Meet Eve. Eve, meet Ed."

Eve Bookman gave me a smile but not a hand. "Glad to meet you at last, Edward. Oliver's talked quite a bit about you." I hoped she was just being polite in making the latter statement.

I gave her a smile back. "Hope he didn't say anything bad about me. But maybe he did; I was probably a pretty obstreperous brat when he saw me last. I would have been — let's see —"

"Five," said Ollie. "Well, what are we waiting for? Ed, you want we should go right home? Or should we drop in somewhere on the way and hoist a few? You weren't much of a drinker when I knew you last but maybe by now —"

Eve interrupted him. "Let's go home, Oliver. You'll want a nightcap there in any case, and you know you're not supposed to have more than one or two a day. Did he tell you, Edward, about his heart trouble in any of his letters?"

Ollie saved me again. "No, but it's not important. All right, though. We'll head home and I'll have my daily one or two, or maybe, since this is an occasion, three. Ed, is that your suitcase back by where you were sitting?"

I said it was and went back and got it, then went with them to the parking area and to a beautiful cream-colored Buick convertible with the top down. Ollie opened the door for Eve and then held it open after she got in. "Go on, Ed. We can all sit in the front seat." He grinned. "Eve's got an MG and loves to drive it, but we couldn't bring it tonight. With those damn bucket seats, you can't ride three in the whole car." I got in and he went around and got in the driver's side. I was wishing that I could drive it—I'd never piloted a recent Buick—but I couldn't think of any reasonable excuse for offering.

Half an hour later, I wished that I'd not only offered but had insisted. Ollie Bookman was a poor driver. Not a fast driver or a dangerous one, just sloppy. The way he grated gears made my teeth grate with them and his starts and stops were much too jerky. Besides, he was a lane-straddler and had no sense of timing on making stop lights.

But he was a good talker. He talked almost incessantly, and to good purpose, briefing me, mostly by apparently talking to Eve. "Don't remember if I told you, Eve, how come Ed and I have different last names, but the same father—not the same mother. See, I was Dad's son by his first marriage and Ed by his second—Ed was born Ed Bookman. But Dad died right after Ed was born and Ed's mother, my stepmother, married Wilkes Cartwright a couple years later. Ed was young enough that they changed his name to match his stepfather's, but I was already grown up, through high school anyway, so I didn't change mine. I was on my own by then. Well, both Ed's mother and his stepfather are dead now; he and I are the only survivors. Well . . ." And I listened and filed away facts. Sometimes he'd cut me in by asking me questions, but the questions always cued in their own answers or were ones that wouldn't be giveaways whichever way I answered them, like, "Ed, the house you were born in, out north of town—is it still standing, or haven't you been out that way recently?"

I was fairly well keyed in on family history by the time we got home.

5

Home wasn't as I'd pictured it, a house. It was an apartment, but a big one—ten rooms, I learned later—on Coleman Boulevard just north of Howard. It was fourth floor, but there were elevators. Now that I thought of it, I realized that Ollie, because of his angina, wouldn't be able to live in a house where he had to climb stairs. But later I learned they'd been living there ever since they'd married, so he hadn't had to move there on account of that angle.

It was a fine apartment, nicely furnished and with a living room big enough to contain a swimming pool. "Come on, Ed," Ollie said cheerfully. "I'll show you your room and let you get rid of your suitcase, freshen up if you want to—although I imagine we'll all be turning in soon. You must be tired after that long trip. Eve, could we talk you into making a round of Martinis meanwhile?"

"Yes, Oliver." The perfect wife, she walked toward the small but well-stocked bar in a corner of the room.

I followed Ollie to the guest room that was to be mine. "Might as well unpack your suitcase while we talk," he said, after he closed the door behind us. "Hang your stuff up or put it in the dresser there. Well, so far, so good. Not a suspicion, and you're doing fine."

"Lots of questions I've still got to ask you, Ollie. We shouldn't take time to talk much now, but when will we have a chance to?"

"Tomorrow. I'll say I have to go downtown, make up some reasons. And you've got your excuse already—the business you came to do. Maybe you can get it over with sooner than you thought — but then decide, since you've come this far anyway, to stay out the week. That way you can stick around here as much as you want, or go out only when I go out."

"Fine. We'll talk that out tomorrow. But about tonight, we'll be talking, the three of us, and what can I safely talk about? Does she know anything about the size of my business, or can I improvise freely and talk about it?"

"Improvise your head off. I've never talked about your business. Don't know much about it myself."

"Good. Another question. How come, at only twenty-five, I've got a business of my own? Most people are still working for somebody else at that age."

"You inherited it from your stepfather, Cartwright. He died three years ago. You were working in the shop and moved to the office and took over. And as far as I know, or Eve, you're doing okay with it."

"Good. And I'm not married?"

"No, but if you want to invent a girl you're thinking about marrying, that's another safe thing you can improvise about."

I put the last of the contents of my suitcase in the dresser drawer and we went back to the living room. Eve had the cocktails made and was waiting for us. We sat around sipping at them, and this time I was able to do most of the talking instead of having to let Ollie filibuster so I wouldn't put my foot into my mouth by saying something wrong.

Ollie suggested a second round but Eve stood up and said that she was tired and that if we'd excuse her, she'd retire. And she gave Ollie a wifely caution about not having more than one more drink. He promised he wouldn't and made a second round for himself and me.

He yawned when he put his down after the first sip. "Guess this will be the last one, Ed. I'm tired, too. And we'll have plenty of time to talk tomorrow."

I wasn't tired, but if he was, that was all right by me. We finished our nightcaps fairly quickly.

"My room's the one next to yours," he told me as he took our glasses back to the bar. "No connecting door, but if you want anything, rap on the wall and I'll hear you. I'm a light sleeper."

"So am I," I told him. "So make it vice versa on the rapping. I'm the one that's supposed to be protecting you, not the other way around."

"And Eve's room is the one on the other side of mine. No connecting door there, either. Not that I'd use it, at this stage, even if it stood wide open with a red carpet running through it."

"She's still a beautiful woman," I said, just to see how he'd answer it.

"Yes. But I guess I'm by nature monogamous. And this may sound corny and be corny, but I consider Dorothy and me married in the sight of God. She's all I'll ever want, she and the boy. Well, come on, and we'll turn in."

I turned in, but I didn't go right to sleep. I lay awake thinking, sorting out my preliminary impressions. Eve Bookman—yes, I believed Ollie's story about their marriage and didn't even think it was exaggerated. Most people would think her sexy as hell to look at her, but I've got a sort of radar when it comes to sexiness. It hadn't registered with a single blip on the screen. And Koslovsky is a much better than average judge of people and what had he said about her? Oh, yes, he'd called her a cold potato.

Some women just naturally hate sex and men—and some of those very women become things like strip teasers because it gives them pleasure to arouse and frustrate men. If one of them breaks down and has an affair with a man, it's because the man has money, as Ollie had, and she thinks she can hook him for a husband, as Eve did Ollie. And once she's got him safely hog-tied, he's on his own and she can be her sweet, frigid self again. True, she's given up the privilege of frustrating men in audience-size groups, but she can torture the hell out of one man, as long as he keeps wanting her, and achieve respectability and even social position while she's doing it.

Oh, she'd been very pleasant to me, very hospitable, and no doubt was pleasant to all of Ollie's friends. And most of them, the ones without radar, probably thought she was a ball of fire in bed and that Ollie was a very lucky guy.

But murder—I was going to take some more convincing on that. It could be Ollie's imagination entirely. The only physical fact he'd come up with to indicate even the possibility of it was the business of the missing will. And she could have taken and destroyed that but still have no intention of killing him before he could make another like it; she could simply be hoping he'd never discover that it was missing.

But I could be wrong, very wrong. I'd met Eve less than three hours ago and Ollie had lived with her eight years. Maybe there was more than met the eye. Well, I'd keep my eyes open and give Ollie a run for his five hundred bucks by not assuming that he was making a murder out of a molehill. I went to sleep and Ollie didn't tap on my wall.

6

I woke at seven but decided that would be too early and that I didn't want to make a nuisance of myself by being up and around before anybody else, so I went back to sleep and it was half past nine when I woke the second time. I got up, showered and shaved—my bedroom had a private bath so all of them must have—dressed and went exploring. I went back to the living room and through it, and found a dining room. The table was set for breakfast for three but no one was there yet.

A matronly-looking woman who'd be a cook or housekeeper— I later learned that she was both and her name was Mrs. Ledbetter—appeared in the doorway that led through a pantry to the kitchen and smiled at me. "You must be Mr. Bookman's brother," she said. "What would you like for breakfast?"

"What time do the Bookmans come down for breakfast?" I asked.

"Usually earlier than this. But I guess you talked late last night. They should be up soon, though."

"Then I won't eat alone, thanks. I'll wait till at least one of them shows up. And as for what I want—anything; whatever they will be having. I'm not fussy about breakfasts."

She smiled and disappeared into the kitchen and I disappeared into the living room. I took a chair with a magazine rack beside it and was leafing through the latest *Reader's Digest,* just reading the short items in it, when Ollie came in looking rested and cheerful. "Morning, Ed. Had breakfast?"

I told him I'd been up only a few minutes and had decided to wait for company. "Come on, then," he said. "We won't wait for Eve. She might be dressing now, but then again she might sleep till noon."

But she didn't sleep till noon; she came in when we were starting our coffee, and told Mrs. Ledbetter that she'd just have coffee, as she had a lunch engagement in only two hours. So the three of us sat drinking coffee and it was very cozy and you wouldn't have guessed there was a thing wrong. You wouldn't have guessed it, but you might have felt it. Anyway, I felt it.

Ollie asked me if I wanted a lift downtown to do the business I'd come to do, and of course I said that I did. We discussed plans. Mrs. Ledbetter, I learned, had the afternoon and evening off, starting at noon, so no dinner would be served that evening. Eve would be gone all afternoon, playing bridge after her lunch date, and she suggested we all meet in the Loop and have dinner there. I wasn't supposed to know Chicago, of course, so I let them pick the place and it came up the Pump Room at seven.

Ollie and I left and on the way to the garage back of the building, I asked him if he minded if I drove the Buick. I said I liked driving and didn't get much chance to.

"Sure, Ed. But you mean you and Am don't have a car?"

I told him we wanted one but hadn't got around to affording it as yet. The few times we needed one for work, we rented one and simply got by without one for pleasure.

The Buick handled wonderfully. With me behind the wheel, it shifted smoothly, didn't jerk in starting or stopping; it timed stop lights and didn't straddle lanes. I asked how much it cost and said I hoped we'd be able to afford one like it someday. Except that we'd want a sedan because a convertible is too noticeable to use for a tail job. When we rented cars, we usually got a sedan in some neutral color like gray. Detectives used to use black cars, but nowadays a black car is almost as conspicuous as a red one.

I asked Ollie where he wanted me to drive him and he said he'd like to go to see Dorothy Stark and his son, Jerry. They lived in an apartment on LaSalle near Chicago Avenue. And did I have any plans or would I like to come up to meet them? He said he would like that.

I told him I'd drop up briefly if he wanted me to, but that I had plans. I wanted him to lend me the key to his apartment and I was going back there, after I could be sure both Mrs. Ledbetter and Mrs. Bookman had left. Since it was the former's afternoon off, it would be the best chance I'd have to look around the place in privacy. He said sure, the key was on the ring with the car keys and I might as well keep the keys, car and all, until our dinner date at the Pump Room. It would be only a short cab ride for him to get there from Mrs. Stark's. I asked him if there was any danger that Eve would go back to the apartment after her lunch date and before her bridge game. He was almost sure she wouldn't, but her bridge club broke up about five thirty and she'd probably go back then to dress for dinner. That was all right; I could be gone by then.

When I parked the car on LaSalle, I remembered to ask him who I was supposed to be when I met Mrs. Stark—Ed Hunter or Ed Cartwright. He suggested we stick to the Cartwright story; if he told Dorothy the truth, she'd worry about him being in danger. Anyway, it would be simpler and take less explanation.

I liked Dorothy Stark on sight. She was small and brunette, with a heart-shaped face. Only passably pretty—nowhere near as stunning as Eve—but she was warm and genuine, the real thing. And really in love with Ollie; I didn't need radar to tell me that. And Jerry, age two, was a cute toddler. I can take kids or let them alone, but Ollie was nuts about him.

I stayed only half an hour, breaking away with the excuse of having a business-lunch date in the Loop, but it was a very pleasant half hour, and Ollie was a completely different person here. He was at home in this small apartment, much more so than in the large apartment on Coleman Boulevard. And you had the feeling that Dorothy was his wife, not Eve.

I was only a half a dozen blocks from the office and I didn't want to get out to Coleman Boulevard before one o'clock, so I drove over to State Street and went up to see if Uncle Am was there. He was, and I told him what little I'd learned to date and what my plans were.

"Kid," he said, "I'd like a ride in that chariot you're pushing. How about us having an early lunch and then I'll go out with you and help search the joint. Two of us can do twice as good a job."

It was tempting but I thumbed it down. If a wheel did come off and Eve Bookman came back unexpectedly, I could give her a song and dance as to what I was doing there, but Uncle Am would be harder to explain. I said I'd give him the ride, though. We could leave now and he could come with me out as far as Howard Avenue and we'd eat somewhere out there; then he could take the el back south from the Howard station. It would amount only to his taking a two-hour lunch break and we did that any time we felt like it. He liked the idea.

I let him drive the second half of the way and he fell in love with the car, too. After we had lunch, I phoned the apartment from the restaurant and let the phone ring a dozen times to make sure both Mrs. Bookman and Mrs. Ledbetter were gone. Then I drove Uncle Am to the el station and myself to the apartment.

7

I let myself in and put the chain on the door. If Eve came back too soon, that was going to be embarrassing to explain; I'd have to say I'd done it absent-mindedly and it would make me look like a fool. But it would be less embarrassing than to have her walk in and find me rooting in the drawers of her dresser.

First, I decided, I'd take a look at the place as a whole. The living room, dining room, and the guest bedroom were the only rooms I'd been in thus far. I decided to start at the back. I went through the dining room and the pantry into the kitchen. It was a big kitchen and had the works in the way of equipment, even an automatic dishwasher and garbage disposal. A room on one side of it was a service and storage room and on the other side was a bedroom; Mrs. Ledbetter's, of course. I looked around in all three rooms but didn't touch anything. I went back to the dining room and found that a door from it led to a room probably intended as a den or study; there was a desk—an old-fashioned roll-top desk that was really an antique—two file cabinets, a bookcase filled mostly with books on construction and business practice but with a few novels on one shelf, mostly mysteries, a typewriter on a stand, and a dictating machine. This was Ollie's office, from which he conducted whatever business he still did. And the dictating machine meant he must have a part-time secretary, however many days or hours a week. He'd hardly dictate letters and then transcribe them himself.

The roll-top desk was closed but not locked. I opened it and saw a lot of papers and envelopes in pigeonholes, but I didn't study any of them. Ollie's business was no business of mine. But I wondered if he'd used the "Purloined Letter" method of hiding his missing will by having it in plain sight in one of those pigeonholes. And if so, what had Eve been looking for when she found it? I made a mental note to ask him about that.

There was a telephone on top of the desk and I looked at the number on it; it wasn't the same number as that on the phone in the living room, which meant it wasn't an extension but a private line.

I closed the desk and went back to the living room and through its side doorway to the hall from which the bedrooms opened. Another door from it turned out to be a linen closet.

Ollie's bedroom was the same size as mine and furnished in the same way. I walked over to the dresser. A little bottle on it contained nitroglycerin pills. It held a hundred and was about half full. Beside it were three glass ampoules of amyl nitrite like the one in my pocket, the one I'd got from Doc Kruger last night at dinner. I looked at the ampoules and decided that they hadn't been tampered with. Couldn't be tampered with, in fact. But I took a couple of the nitro pills out of the bottle and put them in my pocket. If I had a chance to get them to Uncle Am, I'd ask him to take them to a laboratory and have them checked to make sure they were really what the label claimed them to be.

I didn't search the room thoroughly, but I looked through the dresser drawers and the closet. I wasn't sure what I was looking for, unless maybe a gun. If Ollie kept a gun, I wanted to know it. But I didn't find a gun or anything else more dangerous than a nail file.

Eve Bookman's room was, of course, the main object of my search, but I wasn't in any hurry and decided I'd do a little thinking before I tackled it. I went back to the living room and since it occurred to me that if Eve was coming back between lunch and bridge, this would be about the time, I took the chain off the door. It wouldn't matter if I was found here, as long as I was innocently occupied. I could just say that I was unable to see the man I'd come to see until tomorrow. And that Ollie—Oliver to her—had had things to do in the Loop and had lent me his car and his house key.

I made myself a highball at the bar and sat down to sip it and think, but the thinking didn't get me anywhere. I knew one thing I'd be looking for—pills the size and color of nitro pills but that might turn out to be something else. Or a gun or any other lethal weapon, or poison—if it could be identified as such. But that was all and it didn't seem very likely to me that I'd find any of those things, even if Eve did have any designs on her husband's life. One other thing I thought of: I might as well finish my search for a gun by looking for one in Ollie's office. If he had one, I wanted to know it, and he might keep it in his study instead of his bedroom.

I made myself another short drink and did some more thinking without getting any ideas except that if I could reach Ollie by phone at the Stark apartment, I could simply ask him about the gun, and another question or two I'd thought of.

I rinsed out and wiped the glass I'd used and went to the telephone. I checked the book and found a *Stark, Dorothy* on LaSalle Street and called the number. Ollie answered and when I asked him if he could talk freely, he said sure, that Dorothy had gone out shopping and had left him to baby-sit.

I asked him about guns and he said no, he didn't own any.

I told him I'd noticed the ampoules and pills on his dresser and asked him if he carried some of both with him. He said the pills yes, always. But he didn't carry ampoules because the pills always worked for him and the ampoules he just kept on hand at home in case his angina should get worse. He told me the same thing about them the doctor had, that if one used them often they became ineffective. He'd used one only once thus far, and wouldn't again until and unless he had to.

After I'd hung up, I remembered that I'd forgotten to ask him where the will had been hidden in his office but it didn't seem worth while calling back to ask him. I wanted to know, if only out of curiosity, but there wasn't any hurry and I could find out the next time I talked to him alone.

I put the chain bolt back on the door—I was pretty sure by now that Eve wasn't coming back before her bridge-club session, as it was already after two, but I thought I might as well play safe—and went to her room.

8

It was bigger than any of the other bedrooms—had originally, no doubt, been intended as the master bedroom—and it had a dressing room attached and lots of closet space. It was going to be a lot of territory to cover thoroughly, but if Eve had any secrets, they'd surely be here, not in Ledbetter territory like the kitchen or Ollie's office or neutral territory like the living room. Apparently she spent a lot of time here; besides the usual bedroom furniture and a vanity table, there was a bookcase of novels and a writing desk that looked used. I sighed and pitched in. Two hours later, all I knew that I hadn't known—but might have suspected— before was that a woman can have more clothes and more beauty preparations than a man would think possible.

I'd looked in everything but the writing desk; I'd saved that for last. There were three drawers and the top one contained only raw materials—paper and envelopes, pencils, ink and such. No pens, but she probably used a fountain pen and carried it with her. The middle one contained canceled checks, neatly in order and rubber-banded, used stubs of checkbooks similarly banded, and bank statements. No current checkbook; she must have had it with her. The bottom drawer was empty except for a dictionary, a Merriam-Webster *Collegiate.* If she corresponded with anyone, beyond sending out checks to pay bills, she must have destroyed letters when she answered them and not owed any at the moment; there was no correspondence at all.

I still had almost an hour of safe time, since her bridge club surely wouldn't break up before five, so for lack of anything else to go through, I started studying the bank statements and the canceled checks. One thing was immediately obvious: this was her personal account, for clothes and other personal expenses. There was one deposit a month for exactly four hundred dollars, never more or never less. None of the checks drawn against this account would have been for household expenses. Ollie must have handled them, or had his hypothetical part-time secretary (that was another thing I hadn't remembered to ask him about, but again it was nothing I was in a hurry to know) handle them. This account was strictly a personal one. Some of the checks, usually twenty-five- or fifty-dollar ones, were drawn to cash. Others, most of them for odd amounts, were made out to stores. There was one every month to a Howard Avenue Drugstore, no doubt mostly for cosmetics; most of the others were to clothing stores, lingerie shops and the like. Occasional checks to some woman or other for odd amounts up to twenty or thirty dollars were, I decided, probably bridge losses or the like, at times when she didn't have enough cash to pay off. From the bank statements I could see that she lived up to the hilt of her allowance; at the time each four-hundred-dollar check was deposited, always on the first of the month, the balance to which it was added was never over twenty or thirty dollars.

I went through the stack of canceled checks once more. I didn't know what I was looking for, but my subconscious must have noticed something my conscious mind had missed. It had. Not many of the checks were over a hundred dollars, but all of the checks to one outfit, Vogue Shops, Inc., were over a hundred and some were over two hundred. At least half of Eve's four hundred dollars a month was being spent in one place. And other checks were dated at different times, but the Vogue checks were all dated the first of the month exactly. Wondering how much they did total, I took paper and pencil and added the amounts of six of them, for the first six months of the previous year. The smallest was $165.50 and the largest $254.25, but the total — it jarred me. The total of the six checks came to $1,200. Exactly. Even. On the head. And so, I knew a minute later, did the six checks for the second half of the year. It certainly couldn't be coincidence, twice.

Eve Bookman was paying somebody an even two hundred bucks a month — and disguising the fact, on the surface at any rate, by making some of the amounts more than that and some less, but making them average out. I turned over some of the checks to look at the endorsements. Each one was rubber-stamped *Vogue Shops, Inc.,* and under the rubber stamp was the signature *John L. Littleton.* Rubber stamps under that showed they'd all been deposited or cashed at the Dearborn Branch of the Chicago Second National Bank.

And that, whatever it meant, was all the checks were going to tell me. I rebanded them and put them back as I'd found them, took a final look around the room to see that I was leaving everything else as I'd found it, and went back to the living room. I was going to call Uncle Am at the office — if he wasn't there, I could reach him later at the rooming house — but I took the chain off the door first. If Eve walked in while I was talking on the phone, I'd just have to switch the subject of conversation to printing equipment, and Uncle Am would understand.

He was still at the office. I talked fast and when I finished, he said, "Nice going, kid. You've got something by the tail and I'll find out what it is. You stick with the Bookmans and let me handle everything outside. We've got two lucky breaks on this. One, it's Friday and that bank will be open till six o'clock. Two, one of the tellers is a friend of mine. When I get anything for sure, I'll get in touch with you. Is there an extension on the phone there that somebody could listen in on?"

"No," I said. "There's another phone in Ollie's office, but it's a different line."

"Fine, then I can call openly and ask for you. You can pretend it's a business call, if anyone's around, and argue price on a Miehle vertical for your end of the conversation."

"Okay. One other thing." I told him about the two alleged nitro pills I'd appropriated from Ollie's bottle. I told him that on my way in to town for dinner, I'd drop them off on his desk at the office and sometime tomorrow he could take them to the lab. Or maybe, if nitro had a distinctive taste, Doc Kruger could tell by touching one of them to his tongue.

9

It was five o'clock when I hung up the phone. I decided that I'd earned a drink and helped myself to a short one at the bar. Then I went to my room, treated myself to a quick shower and a clean shirt for the evening.

I was just about to open the door to leave when it opened from the other side and Eve Bookman came home. She was pleasantly surprised to find me and I told her how I happened to have the house key and Ollie's car, but said I'd been there only half an hour, just to clean up and change shirts for the evening.

She asked why, since it was five thirty already, I didn't stay and drive her in in Ollie's car. That way we wouldn't be stuck, after dinner, with having both the Buick and the MG downtown with us and could all ride home together.

I told her it sounded like an excellent idea. Which it was, except for the fact that I wanted to get the pills to Uncle Am.

But there was a way around that. I asked if she could give me a piece of paper, envelope and stamp. She went to her room to get them and after she'd gone back there to dress, I addressed the envelope to Uncle Am at the office, folded the paper around the pills and sealed them in the envelope. All I'd have to do was mail it, on our way in, at the Dearborn Post Office Station and it would get there in the morning delivery.

I made myself comfortable with a magazine to read and Eve surprised me by taking not too long to get ready. And she looked gorgeous, and I told her so, when she came back to the living room. It was only six fifteen and I didn't have to speed to get us to the Pump Room by seven. Ollie wasn't there, but he'd reserved us a table and left word with the maître d' that something had come up and he'd be a bit late.

He was quite a bit late and we were finishing our third round of Martinis when he showed up, very apologetic about being detained. We decided we'd have one more so he could have one with us, and then ate a wonderful meal. As an out-of-town guest who was presuming on their hospitality already, I insisted on grabbing the check. A nice touch, since it would go on Ollie's bill anyway.

We discussed going on to a night club, but Eve said that Ollie looked tired—which he did—and if we went clubbing, would want to drink too much. We could have a drink or two at home—if Ollie would promise to hold to two. He said he would.

Since Ollie admitted that he really was a little tired, I had no trouble talking him into letting me do the driving again. Eve seemed more genuinely friendly than hitherto. Maybe it was the Martinis before dinner or maybe she was getting to like me. But it was an at-a-distance type of friendliness; my radar told me that.

Back home, I offered to do the bartending, but Eve overruled me and made our drinks. We were drinking them and talking about nothing in particular when I saw Ollie suddenly put down his glass and bend forward slightly, putting his right hand under his left arm.

Then he straightened up and saw that we were both looking at him with concern. He said, "Nothing. Just a little twinge, not an attack. But maybe to be on the safe side, I'll take one—"

He took a little gold pillbox out of his pocket and opened it.

"Good Lord," he said, standing up. "Forgot I took my last one just before I got to the Pump Room. Just as well we didn't go night-clubbing, after all. Well, it's okay now. I'll fill it."

"Let me—" I said.

But he looked perfectly well now and waved me away. "I'm perfectly okay. Don't worry."

And he went into the hallway, walking confidently, and I heard the door of his room open and close so I knew he'd made it all right.

Eve started to make conversation by asking me questions about the girl in Seattle whom I'd talked about, and I was answering and enjoying it, when suddenly I realized Ollie had been gone at least five minutes and maybe ten. A lot longer than it would take to refill a pillbox. Of course he might have decided to go to the john or something while he was there, but just the same, I stood up quickly, excused myself without explaining, headed for his room.

The minute I opened the door, I saw him and thought he was dead. He was lying face down on the rug in front of the dresser and on the dresser there wasn't any little bottle of pills and there weren't any amyl nitrite ampoules, either.

I bent over him, but I didn't waste time trying to find out whether he was dead or not. If he was, the ampoule I'd got from Doc Kruger wasn't going to hurt him. And if he was alive, a fraction of a second might make the difference of whether it would save him or not. I didn't feel for a heartbeat or look at his face. I got hold of a handful of hair and lifted his head a few inches off the floor, reached in under it with my hand and crushed the ampoule right under his nose.

Eve was standing in the doorway and I barked at her to phone for an ambulance, right away quick. She ran back toward the living room.

10

Ollie didn't die, although he certainly would have if I hadn't had the bright idea of appropriating that ampoule from Doc and carrying it with me. But Ollie was in bad shape for a while, and Uncle Am and I didn't get to see him until two days later, Sunday evening.

His face looked gray and drawn and he was having to lie very quiet. But he could talk, and they gave us fifteen minutes with him. And they'd told us he was definitely out of danger, as long as he behaved himself, but he'd still be in the hospital another week or maybe even two.

But bad as he looked, I didn't pull any punches. "Ollie," I said, "it didn't work, your little frame-up. I didn't go to the police and accuse Eve of trying to murder you. On the other hand, I've given you this break, so far. I didn't go to them and tell them you tried to commit suicide in a way to frame her for murder. You must love Dorothy and Jerry awfully much to have planned that."

"I—I do," he said. "What—made you guess, Ed?"

"Your hands, for one thing," I said. "They were dirtier than they'd have been if you'd just fallen. That and the fact that you were lying face down told me how you managed to bring on that attack at just that moment. You were doing push-ups—about as strenuous and concentrated exercise as a man can take. And just kept doing them till you passed out. It *should* have been fatal, all right.

"And you knew the pills and ampoules had been on your dresser that afternoon, and that Eve had been home since I'd seen them and could have taken them. Actually you took them yourself. You came out in a taxi—and we could probably find the taxi if we had to prove this—and got them yourself. You had to wait till you were sure Eve and I would be en route downtown, and that's why you were so late getting to the Pump Room. Now Uncle Am's got news for you—not that you deserve it."

Uncle Am cleared his throat. "You're not married, Ollie. You're a free man because your marriage to Eve Packer wasn't legal. She'd been married before and hadn't got a divorce. Probably because she had no intention of marrying again until you popped the question to her, and then it was too late to get one.

"Her legal husband, who left her ten years ago, is a bartender named Littleton. He found her again somehow and when he learned she'd married you illegally, he started blackmailing her. She's been paying him two hundred a month, half the pinmoney allowance you gave her, for three years. They worked out a way she could mail him checks and still have her money seemingly accounted for. The method doesn't matter."

I took over. "We haven't called copper on the bigamy bit, either, because you're not going to prosecute her for it, or tell the cops. We figure you owe her something for having tried to frame her on a murder charge. We've talked to her. She'll leave town quietly, and go to Reno, and in a little while you can let out that you're divorced and free. And marry Dorothy and legitimize Jerry.

"She really will be getting a divorce, incidentally, but from Littleton, not from you. I said you'd finance that and give her a reasonable stake to start out with. Like ten thousand dollars— does that sound reasonable?"

He nodded. His face looked less drawn, less gray now. I had a hunch his improvement would be a lot faster now.

"And you fellows," he said. "How can I ever—?"

"We're even," Uncle Am said. "Your retainer will cover. But don't ever look us up again to do a job for you. A private detective doesn't like to be made a patsy, be put in the spot of helping a frame-up. And that's what you tried to do to us. Don't ever look us up again."

We never saw Ollie again, but we did hear from him once, a few months later. One morning, a Western Union messenger came into our office to deliver a note and a little box. He said he had instructions not to wait and left.

The envelope contained a wedding announcement. One of the after-the-fact kind, not an invitation, of the marriage of Oliver R. Bookman to Dorothy Stark. On the back of it was scribbled a note. "Hope you've forgiven me enough to accept a wedding present in reverse. I've arranged for the dealer to leave it out front. Papers will be in glove compartment. Thanks for everything, including accepting this." And the little box, of course, contained two sets of car keys.

It was, as I'd known it would be, a brand-new Buick sedan, gray, a hell of a car. We stood looking at it, and Uncle Am said, "Well, Ed, have we forgiven him enough?"

"I guess so," I said. "It's a sweet chariot. But somebody got off on his time, either the car dealer or the messenger, and it's been here too long. Look."

I pointed to the parking ticket on the windshield. "Well, shall we take our first ride in it, down to the City Hall to pay the fine and get right with God?"

We did.

A CAT WALKS

It all started with one cat, one small gray cat. It ended with nine of them. Gray cats all—because at night all cats are gray—and some of them were alive and others dead. And there was a man without a face, but the cats didn't do that.

It started at ten o'clock in the morning. Miss Weyburn must have been waiting for the shop to open, because she came in as soon as I'd put up the shades and unlocked the door. I knew her name was Miss Weyburn because she'd given it to me three days before when she'd come in to leave her cat with us. And she was such a honey that I remembered her name almost as well as I remembered my own or that of the shop. Incidentally, it's the Bon Ton Pet Shop, and I think it's a silly name myself, but my mother has a half interest in it, and you know how women are. It was all I could do to keep it from being a pet *shoppe,* and to avoid that I settled for the Bon Ton part with scarcely more of a murmur than would have caused the neighbors to send in a riot call.

I smiled at her and said, "Good morning, Miss Weyburn."

She had one of our business cards in her hand and said, "Good morning, Mr.—"

She sort of glanced at the card, so I put in quickly: "Don't let the name on the card fool you; I'm not Bon Ton. The name is Phil Evans. Very much at your service. And I hope that—"

"I came to get my cat, please."

I nodded, and stalled. "I remember; you left a cat to be boarded while you were out of town, didn't you? I'm very fond of cats, myself. So many people prefer dogs, but there's something about a cat—a kind of quiet dignity and self-respect. Dogs seem to lack it. They're boisterous and haven't any subtlety. They—"

"I would like," she said firmly, "to have my cat. Now. To take out."

"Yes, ma'am; with or without mustar— Now, don't get mad! Please. I'll get it. Let's see; it was a small gray cat, I recall. I presume you want the same one. What is its name?"

And then the way she was looking at me made me decide that I'd better get it for her right away and try to resume the conversation afterward. So I went to the back room where we keep most of the pets, and went to the cage where Miss Weyburn's cat had been.

The cage was empty. The door was closed and latched, so it couldn't have got out by itself. But it wasn't there.

Incredulously, I opened the door of the cage to look in; which was silly, because I could see through the netting perfectly well that the cage was empty.

And so were the cages on either side. In fact, Miaow Alley— the row of cat cages—was a deserted street. There weren't any cats. Neither Miss Weyburn's nor the four other cats, our own cats, which had been there yesterday.

I looked around the room quickly, but everything else was O.K. I mean, all the dogs were there, and the canaries chirping as usual, and the big parrot that we have to keep out of sight in the back room until he's forgotten a few of the words somebody taught him.

But there weren't any cats.

I was too surprised, just then, to be worried. I went to the

A CAT WALKS

staircase between the back room and the store, and yelled up, "Hey, ma!" and she came to the head of the stairs.

The girl up front said, "Is something wrong with Cinder, Mr. . . . uh . . . Evans?"

I smiled at her reassuringly, or tried to. I said, "Not at all. I . . . I just don't know which cage my mother put him in."

Ma was coming down the stairs and I said to her, "Listen, ma, when you fed the cats this morning, did you—"

"Cats? Why, Phil, there aren't any cats. I told you at breakfast, while you were reading that paper, that you'd have to arrange to get some. Weren't you even listening?"

"But, ma! That little gray cat! It wasn't ours; surely you didn't—"

"Not ours? Why, I thought you told me—"

By that time she was in the store, and she caught the stricken look on Miss Weyburn's face, and got the idea. Meanwhile, I was deciding that I'd never again read at the table while ma was talking to me and sometimes answer "Uh-huh" without being sure what she was saying. But that good resolution wasn't doing any good right at the moment.

Our customer was getting white around the gills and red around the eyes, and her voice sounded like she was trying to keep from crying and wouldn't succeed much longer. She said, "But how *could* you have—" And she was looking at me, and I had to stand there and look back because there wasn't any mouse hole around for me to crawl into.

I gulped. "Miss Weyburn, it looks like we've . . . I've pulled an awful boner. But we'll find that cat and get it back for you. Somehow. Ma, do you know who you sold it to? Was there a sales slip or anything?"

Ma shook her head slowly. "No, the man paid cash. For all of them. And he was such an odd-looking—"

"All of them?" I echoed. "You mean one guy bought all our cats?"

"Yes, Phil. I told you, at breakfast. It was late yesterday afternoon, after you left at four o'clock. You got home so late last night that I didn't have a chance to tell you until—"

"But, ma, what would one guy want with five cats? We had four besides Miss Weyburn's. Did he say what he wanted them for?"

Ma leaned her elbows on the counter. "He wanted a dozen," she said. "Like I told you. And he said he had a big farm and it was overrun with field mice, and that he liked cats and decided to get several of them while he was at it."

I looked at her aghast. "The Siamese? Don't tell me he paid twenty-five bucks for that Siamese to hunt mice on a farm?"

"Phil, you know that cat was only three-quarters Siamese," said ma, "and that you told me to take fifteen, or even less, if we could get it. And the others were all ordinary cats, and he offered twenty-five for the five of them and I took it."

"But haven't you any idea who he was, or where his farm is, or anything about him?"

"Hm-m-m," said ma thoughtfully. "He said his name was— yes, that was it, Smith. Didn't mention his first name. Nor where he lived. Let's see—he was short and stocky, about the size and build of Mr. Workus, say. But he was bald; he didn't wear a hat. And he had a reddish mustache and wore dark glasses."

"That sounds like a disguise," said Miss Weyburn.

Ma blinked. "Why should anyone disguise himself to buy cats?"

"But, ma," I protested, "there must have been something screwy about the guy. Dark glasses and a name like 'Smith' and— Heck, if he wanted cats for mousing, he could have got 'em for nothing. Why pay a fancy price?"

I turned to our customer. "Listen, Miss Weyburn," I said, "I'll check into this, and I'll find your cat, if it's possible. But if I can't— well, were you awfully attached to it? Or if I got you a beautiful thoroughbred Angora or Siamese kitten, would you be—"

A CAT WALKS 141

Tears were running down her cheeks, and I said hastily, "Please don't cry! If it's that important, I'll find your cat if I have to . . . to go to China for it. And if I don't, you can have our whole store, and —" And me with it, I wanted to say, but it didn't seem the proper time and place to say it.

"I don't want your d-darned store. I want —"

"Listen, ma," I said, "you'll watch the store for the rest of the day, won't you? I'm going out to hunt —"

"Sure, Phil." Ma gave me a knowing look. "But first you go back and finish currying that pony, and let me talk to Miss Weyburn."

I got the idea, because we didn't have a pony to curry. So I made myself scarce out the back door for about ten minutes, and gave ma a chance to stop the girl crying. Ma can talk; she can convince almost anybody of almost anything, and when I came in again the girl wasn't crying, and she looked less mad and more cheerful.

"Well," I said, "if you'll tell me where I can get in touch with you, miss, I'll let you know the minute I find —"

"I'm going with you," she interrupted. And I didn't object to that, at all. I said, "That's swell. I'll get the car out of the garage and bring it around front."

And five minutes later, we were driving downtown. First, we stopped at the offices of the two local newspapers and arranged to put in ads addressed to a Mr. Smith who had purchased five cats the day before.

And then I turned the car down Barclay Street.

"Where are we going now?" Miss Weyburn wanted to know.

"Police station," I told her. "Those personal ads were just in case this Smith guy is what he said he was. But there seems to be a faint smell of fish about a guy wanting a dozen cats, and it's just possible that the police may know of him as a nut, or something."

"But —"

"It won't cost anything to try, will it?" I pointed out. "And Lieutenant Granville is a good friend of mine. If he's in—"

And he was. We walked into his office and I said, "Hi, Hank. This is Miss Weyburn. We wanted to talk about a cat. Her cat. A small gray—"

"Stolen?"

"Well, not exactly. I mean if it was, I'm the one who stole it. I was boarding it for her and it was sold by mistake."

Hank glowered at me. "I got *real* trouble. I'm working on a murder case that happened night before last and there aren't any leads and we're against a blank wall, and you come in and want me to hunt a cat."

"If you're up against a blank wall," I pointed out, quite reasonably, "then there's nothing you can do for the moment, and you might as well be human and listen to us."

"Shut up," said Hank. "Miss Weyburn, if Phil sold a cat that belongs to you, he's responsible. Do you want to bring charges against him?"

"N-no."

Hank looked at me again. "Well, then what *do* you want me to do?"

"You yahoo," I said, "I want you to listen. And then, if possible, be helpful." And before he could interrupt again, I managed to tell him the story.

He looked thoughtful. "Checked the pound yet?"

"Why, no—but why would anyone buy a cat, or cats, and then take them to the pound?"

"Not that, Phil. But the guy might have tried to *get* cats there. You said he originally wanted a dozen. Well, it sounds silly to buy cats by the dozen, but it's not illegal. Anyway, he got only five from you. Maybe he kept on trying, or maybe he'd been to the pound first. Maybe he left his address there."

I nodded. "Thanks," I said. "That might be a lead. Hank, I

A CAT WALKS 143

knew there must be some reason why they made you a detective. We'll go to the pound, and we'll go to Workus' pet shop, too. And meanwhile, if you should happen to hear anything—"

"Sure," Hank agreed. "I'll let you know. And, Miss Weyburn, anytime you want to have this guy here put in jail, just let me know and sign a complaint, and I'll be glad to—"

But I got the girl out before Hank could give her any more ideas, and when we got out of the station, I glanced at my watch and saw that it was after noon.

So we stopped in the restaurant across the street, and when we'd ordered, she asked, "Who is this Mr. Workus you mentioned?"

"He runs the other pet shop in town," I explained. "If this Smith wasn't satisfied with five cats, he probably went there next. Anyway, we'll try."

"And if he didn't leave an address at the pound or at the other pet shop?"

Well, she had me there, but I ducked answering, and tried to keep the conversation on more cheerful topics while we ate.

Hank strolled into the restaurant while we were having coffee, and I motioned him over to a seat at our table. He grinned and said, "Well, any more news on the cat-astrophe?"

"This isn't funny," I told him. "Miss Weyburn is attached to that cat. That beagle I sold you last fall, Hank—would you think it a joke if something happened to it?"

He reddened a bit and said, "Sorry, Miss Weyburn. I didn't mean to—"

"That's all right, lieutenant," she said. "What's the important case you're working on?"

"Guy named Blake. Somebody burglarized the Dean laboratories night before last. Blake was the watchman, and they killed him."

"Laboratories?" I asked. "What'd they steal?"

Hank shook his head. "We haven't made a check-up yet; not thorough enough to tell if anything's gone. But there isn't a single clue. Even the F.B.I. men—" He broke off.

"Huh?" I said. "What would the F.B.I. be doing on a burglary-and-murder case?"

Hank looked uncomfortable. He said. "They aren't here on that. Something else. I didn't mean that the Dean burglary was an F.B.I. case."

"In other words," I suggested, "do I think it will rain tomorrow?"

He grinned sheepishly. "That's the general idea."

By that time the waitress was there to take Hank's order, and Miss Weyburn and I left and headed first for the pound. We drew a blank. They hadn't had any cats for several days. There'd been two inquiries about cats the day before, but both by phone calls, and no record had been made. Nor could the man who'd taken the calls remember any helpful details.

So I headed the car for the far side of town. Pete Workus was alone in his shop when we went in. I knew him only slightly; he'd been in business there only a year or so.

"Hello, Pete," I said. "This is Miss Weyburn. We're trying to trace a man who bought five cats at our place yesterday. He wanted more than that, and I thought maybe he came here."

Workus nodded. "He did. Or anyway, there was a guy here who bought us out of cats, so I suppose it's the same one. I sold him three of them."

"Did he leave a name and address?"

Workus leaned an elbow on the counter and rubbed his chin. "Uh, I guess he gave me his name, but I don't remember. It was a common name, I think."

"Smith?"

"Yeah, I guess that was it. But not his address. Anyway, he doesn't want any more cats, Evans, so you can stop hunting for him. I offered to get him some more, but he figured he had

A CAT WALKS 145

enough with what I sold him. Come to think of it, he mentioned your place; he said he got five from you, and he'd got one somewhere else, and with the three I had, he figured nine would be enough."

"I don't want to sell him any more cats," I said. "What happened is that we sold him one too many, by mistake. Miss Weyburn's cat. And I got to get it back for her."

"Hm-m-m, that's tough. Well, I hope you find him then; but I don't know how to help you."

"Maybe," I suggested, "you can add to the description of him that we have."

Workus closed his eyes to think. "Well, he was maybe five feet seven or eight inches, about a hundred and seventy pounds—"

I nodded. "That fits ma's description. And he wore dark glasses while he was here?"

"Yes, yellowish sun glasses. He didn't wear a hat, and he was bald, and he had a mustache. That's . . . that's all I can remember about him. Say, Evans, while you're here will you take a look at a puppy of mine? I hear you're something of a vet, and maybe you can tell me whether it's got distemper or not."

"Sure," I said. "Be glad to. Where is he?"

"Back this way." He opened the door to the room behind the shop, and I went in after him. I turned around to ask the girl if she minded waiting a few minutes, but she was following us. She said, "May I watch?"

"Sure," I told her, and we followed Workus into the back room.

He was leading the way back past a row of cages when it happened. Up at shoulder height, a small brown monkey arm darted out through the bars of one of the upper cages, and grabbed.

Workus swore suddenly as his hair vanished into the monkey cage. Then, his face a bit red, he said, "Excuse my language, miss. But that's the second time that d-darned monkey caught me napping."

He opened the door of the cage and reached in to recover his toupee, which the now-frightened and jabbering monkey had dropped just behind the bars.

I hadn't known, until now, that Workus wore a toupee; and I'd jumped a bit at the apparent spectacle of a man being scalped. For under the toupee, Workus was completely bald.

"Say," I said, half jokingly and half seriously, "it wasn't by any chance you who bought these cats of ours, was it? If you left off your toupee and hat, and put on dark glasses and a mustache—"

Workus had closed the door of the monkey cage, and was adjusting the toupee on his head. He looked at me strangely. "Are you crazy, Evans? Or joking? Why would I want to do a thing like that?"

"I haven't any idea," I said cheerfully. And I hadn't. But something was beginning to buzz at the back of my mind, and without stopping to think it over, I went on talking. "But one thing does strike me funny. My mother described the mysterious Mr. Smith as being about *your* height and weight. Now what made her say that? She's seen you only a few times in her life. But, in thinking what the man who bought the cats was like, she used your name. Doesn't it seem that it might have been because—sort of subconsciously—she saw through the disguise, and recognized your walk, or your voice, or something?"

Workus was frowning. He said, "Are you accusing me of—"

"I'm not accusing you of anything. If it was you, there's nothing criminal about buying cats. All we want is Miss Weyburn's cat back, and we'll . . . I'll pay for it. That sale wasn't legal, anyway. We can get a writ of replevin for the animal. But I hope we won't have to go to the police."

And having gone that far, I decided to bluff it on out, and added, "Or will we?"

He didn't answer at all for a moment. Then, quite suddenly and surprisingly, he grinned at us. "O.K.," he said. "You win. It

A CAT WALKS 147

was me. And I'll see that you get your cat back, Miss—Weyburn, is it? I'll give you a note to the man who has it, and his address."

He crossed toward the desk at one side of the room, and I turned and looked at Miss Weyburn, and said: "See? The Bon Ton Pet Shop gets results. Even if we have to turn into a detective agency. We get our cat. Like the Northwest—"

But she was looking past me, toward Workus. Suddenly, at the startled look on her face, I whirled around. Workus was holding a gun on us. A .38 automatic that looked like a cannon when seen from the front. He said, "Don't move."

For a moment, I thought he was crazy. But I lifted my hands shoulder-high, and I tried to make my voice calm and reasonable. I said, "What's the idea? In the first place, Workus, you can't get away with this. And in the second—"

"Be quiet, Evans. Listen, I don't want to kill you unless I have to, and if you're reasonable, maybe I won't have to. But I can't let you out of here; you'd go to the police and they just might decide to investigate what you told them. Even if you got your cat back, you might."

"Listen," I said. "What's all this about? Am I crazy, or are you? Why this fuss about cats?"

"If you knew that, I'd have to kill you. Still want to know?"

"Well," I said, "if you put it that way, maybe not. But—about holding us here. How long—"

"Tomorrow. I'm through here, and leaving town after tonight. Tomorrow I won't care what you tell the cops. I'll be clear."

I grunted. "But dammit—" I turned my head toward the girl. "I'm sorry, Miss Weyburn. Looks like I got you in a mess."

She managed a fleeting smile. "It isn't your fault. And—"

The sound of a door opening behind me made me start to turn my head farther around, but Workus' voice barked, "Look this way." And the snick of the safety catch on the automatic backed it up, and I turned.

"You first, Evans," Workus snapped. "Put your hands behind you to be tied."

I obeyed, and somebody behind me did a good job of tying my wrists. Then a blindfold was tied over my eyes and a clean handkerchief from my own pocket used as a gag. When, on instructions, I sat down and leaned back against the wall, my ankles, too, were tied.

Then, after Miss Weyburn had been similarly tied and placed beside me, I heard the footsteps of Workus going back to the store at the front. The other man opened and closed a door, and I heard his steps on stairs, but don't know whether he was going up or down them.

And then, for a long time, nothing happened.

I tried, experimentally, to reach the knots in the cord that bound my wrists, but couldn't touch them, even with the tip of one finger. I might have been able to loosen the cord by rolling around until I found a rough edge somewhere to rub it against, but every ten or fifteen minutes, all afternoon, I'd hear Workus' footsteps coming to the door to look in at us, or coming on into the back room on some errand or other. So, for the present, there was nothing I could do—except wait and hope for the best.

Time passed, but slowly. Very slowly. You'd think that in a spot like that, you'd have enough to worry about to keep you from getting bored. But after an hour or two, you haven't. You can be worried, or afraid, or mad, just so long and no longer. It begins to taper off; an hour or two passes like a year or two, and you begin to wish something would happen, almost anything. Time becomes an unendurable vacuum.

I don't know how long it was before I got the idea of opening communication with the girl beside me in code. But suddenly I thought of the old idea of communicating by taps or touches; one for A, two for B, three for C and so on through the alphabet. If she got the idea—

A CAT WALKS 149

I wriggled over a few inches until my right elbow touched her left. By nudges, I spelled out C-A-N U U-N-D-E-R-S—and she saved me from spelling out the rest of the "understand" by cutting in with Y-E-S.

It was a slow and painful method of communication, and I prefer talking and listening, but it helped pass the time and it didn't matter how slow it was, because we had more time than we knew what to do with. And often we could shorten it by interrupting a question in the middle as soon as there was enough of it to guess the rest.

It didn't take long to find out that neither of us could make any intelligent guess as to the motive and purpose of our captors. We decided that if a reasonable chance of escape should offer itself, we should take it rather than trust too completely to Workus' stated intention to let us go the next day. But that for the present, we'd better make the best of it.

Then—for chivalrous, if unromantic, reasons—I moved farther away from her. I had discovered that I entertained other company. Undoubtedly, I was too near the monkey cage, and undoubtedly Workus was too stingy with his flea powder. I probably got only a couple of them, but they moved around and gave the impression of a legion.

But time did pass, and after a while I heard Workus closing up the shop and pulling down the shades. He didn't leave, though, but remained up front, still looking in on us occasionally. The man who'd gone up or down the stairs rejoined Workus; then first one and then the other left by the back door and returned after a while. Probably they had gone out to eat; one at a time, while the other remained on guard.

After a while my trained fleas seemed to have left me, and it was lonesome alone, so I slid over next to the girl again. I spelled out O-K and tried to figure out how to put a question mark after it and couldn't, but she spelled back Y-E-S W-H-E-R-E W-E-R-E

U, and I spelled F-L-E-A-S, and she came back N-O T-H-A-N-K-S, which didn't make sense, but then probably my answer hadn't made sense to her.

Then — it must have been close to nine o'clock — the two men came into the back room together. One of them took my shoulders and one of them my feet and I was carried out the back door and into what I judged to be Workus' truck; a light delivery van with a closed body. A minute later the girl was put in with me and the back door of the truck closed and latched.

The engine started and I hit my head a resounding thump as the car jerked into motion.

It lurched through the roughly paved alley. Out on the streets, the motion wasn't so bad. But from time to time we hit bumps and went around corners. I tried to brace myself, sitting up and leaning against a side of the truck body, but it didn't work. The only way to avoid frequent head thumpings was to lie flat.

Apparently the girl had made the same discovery, because I found her lying beside me, and we found that by lying close together we minimized the jouncing and rolling. We didn't try our code of signaling, because the joggling of the moving truck would have made it impossible.

After an hour or so the truck hit a rough driveway again, went along it what seemed quite a distance, and stopped. From the time we'd been traveling, I judged that we were well out in the country somewhere; but I couldn't have made the wildest guess as to our direction from town.

Then the ignition went off, and the truck stopped and stood still. I heard the doors on either side of the truck cab slam, but Miss Weyburn was spelling out something by nudging my elbow and I concentrated on that and got: R U A-L-L R-I-T-E, and answered Y-E-S, and then it occurred to me that spelling out that question and answer had taken quite a bit of time, and why hadn't Workus and the other chap opened the back of the truck to take us out?

A CAT WALKS   151

But maybe they weren't going to. Maybe they intended merely to leave us here in the truck while they accomplished their business — whatever it was — in this place, and they'd get rid of us later.

And that meant that we might have quite a bit of time here.

There was one possible way of our getting loose from those all-too-efficiently tied cords around our wrists. A way I'd thought of, but which hadn't been practicable in the back room of Workus' pet shop, with him looking back at us frequently. But now —

As quickly as I could, I spelled out: L-I-E O-N S-I-D-E W-I-L-L T-R-Y U-N-T-I-E.

She got the idea, for instead of trying to answer, she immediately rolled over with her back toward me and held out her bound wrists.

My fingers were almost numb from lack of proper circulation, but I started right in on the knotted cord about her wrists, and the effort of trying to untie it gradually restored my hands to normal.

It was a tough knot; we'd been tied with ordinary heavy wrapping twine, I found. Several turns of it, and then a knot that was made up of four square knots, well tied; each had been pulled as tight as possible before the next one was made.

But one at a time, they gave way. It was slow business, because my own wrists were tied crosswise and I could reach the knots of the girl's bindings with the fingers of only one hand at a time. It must have taken me nearly half an hour before the inner knot gave way and I felt the cord itself slip as she pulled her wrists apart.

A moment later she took off my gag and blindfold and then whispered, "I'll have you loose in a minute, Mr. Evans."

"Phil, now," I whispered back, as she started work on the cords on my wrists. "What's your name?"

"Ellen." With both her hands free, she could make faster progress than I had on her bindings. "Got any idea where we are?"

"No, but it must be way out in the country. No street lights or anything. And listen; isn't that frogs?"

It was dark inside that truck, but when my wrists came free and I sat up to start on the knots at my ankles—while Ellen did the same with hers—I could see a dim, gray square that was the back window of the truck.

"Listen," Ellen said. "Did you hear—"

It was the distant yowling of a cat. Of several cats. Once my ears were attuned to the sound, I could hear it quite plainly.

I whispered, "Is it Cinder? Can you recognize his . . . uh . . . voice?"

"I think so. I'm almost sure. There—my ankles are—"

The cords on my own ankles came loose at the same moment, and I crawled to the back of the truck. The twin doors were latched from the outside, and I reached through the barred window, but I couldn't get enough of my arm through to reach down and turn the handle.

Ellen joined me, and her more slender arm solved the problem.

We stepped down, cautiously, into the unknown. We stood there, listening.

Frogs. Crickets. And cats.

There was a thin sliver of new moon playing hide and seek among high cumulus clouds, fast drifting, although down on the ground there didn't seem to be a breath of wind.

We were standing on grass between two wheel ruts that were a crude sort of driveway. It led, ahead past the front of the truck, to what looked like a big, ramshackle barn.

And a dozen yards the other direction was a building that looked like a farmhouse. An abandoned farmhouse, judging from its state of disrepair and the high grass and weeds about it. There was a dim light in one room that seemed to be the kitchen.

I took Ellen's arm and whispered, "The driveway to the road

A CAT WALKS

leads back past the house. Shall we risk that—or try the other way?"

"You decide. But let's— Isn't that the way the cats are?" She pointed away from the house, out past the dark barn; and the distant caterwauling did seem to come from that direction.

As far as danger was concerned, it seemed a toss-up. Past the house was probably the direction of the nearest road. But if we made a sound as we went by the house, we'd never reach safety. And, too, if they came to the truck and found us gone, that's the direction they'd figure we took.

"This way," I said, and led around the truck and past the barn. It would be farther, that way, to the next road. But we'd have a better chance of making it.

We went around the side of the barn farthest from the house, and on the farther side we came upon a dimly defined path, one that we could barely follow.

We found that the feline serenade grew louder as we progressed. The path led through a brief patch of woods, and then, quite suddenly, started downhill.

It was there that we saw the man without a face. I was in the lead, and I heard footsteps. They seemed to come toward us from the direction in which we were heading. I stopped walking so abruptly that Ellen ran into me, but I grabbed her before she could make a sound.

"Back, and step carefully," I whispered. "Somebody's coming."

We were only a few steps out of the woods through which the path had run, and I led her back to it and then off the path among the trees.

And then, peering from the edge of the woods well to one side of the path, we watched in the direction in which we'd been walking.

There was a moment of comparatively bright moonlight, and in it we saw a man—or something—coming along the path toward us. He was about twenty yards away when we saw him. The figure was tall and thin and seemed to be that of a man, but—well, there just didn't seem to be any face where a face should have been. A blank area with two huge blanked circles that were too large for eyes.

I felt Ellen's fingers constrict suddenly about my arm. And then that damn sliver of moon slid behind clouds again, and we were staring into gray nothingness.

The footsteps paused. There was a faint click and a circle of yellow leaped out on the path. The faceless man had turned on a flashlight, and its beam danced ahead of him as he came on into the woods and passed us. But there wasn't enough reflected light from it to give us another look at whoever held it.

We waited several minutes, not quite daring to whisper, until we were sure that he was well past us back toward the house. Then I said, "Come on, let's get this over with. Unless you'd rather try back the other way?"

She whispered, "No, I'd rather go on this way. Even if it wasn't for Cinder being this way—"

We groped our way back to the path and out of the woods again into the downhill stretch of the path.

We were quite close to the source of the caterwauling now, and I noticed something puzzling. Fewer cats seemed to be making the noise.

Then, quite suddenly, the sliver of moon came out brightly from behind the clouds and, with our eyes accustomed to a greater darkness, we could see comparatively well.

The path leveled off and we were standing on a flat area at the bottom of a valley. Quite near it was a wooden box, an ordinary small crate from a grocery. There were slats nailed across one side to make it into a crude cage. And—if my ears told me aright—there was a cat inside it.

Five feet ahead was another such box, and five feet beyond

that—yes, a whole row of crude soap-box cages, each five feet from the next. Nine of them.

The reappearance of the moon left us standing in the open, and my first impulse was to duck for cover—but there wasn't any in sight. There wasn't any human being in sight, either—fortunately, or we'd have been seen right away.

I heard Ellen gasp, and then she ran past me to the nearest wooden cage. She bent down, and then turned as I joined her. "It isn't Cinder," she said. "But let it out, anyway. I don't know what on earth—"

I didn't know, either. Ellen was going on to the next cage. If we'd used our common sense, we'd have run like hell and come back later, with the police, to rescue the cats. But—well, there we were, and we didn't. I reached down and pulled loose one of the carelessly nailed slats of the box, and a gray streak went past me and vanished.

From the second cage, Ellen said, "Here he is!" and she herself was tearing a slat loose from the box, eagerly. When I got there she was cuddling a small gray cat in her arms, and it snuggled up to her, purring.

"Swell," I said. "Let's get going. We'll come to a farm or a road or something, and— But wait!"

"Phil, those other cats—"

"You're darn right," I told her. "I'm going to let them out first. I don't know why, but—"

It wasn't even a hunch; as yet I hadn't made a guess what it was all about. But it was instinctive; I love animals and I wasn't going to run off and leave seven more cats in those cages. It was quixotic, maybe, to risk sticking around to let them go, but it wouldn't take more than two minutes to do it, and we'd been there longer than that already and nobody had challenged us.

I ran to the next cage and released the cat that was in it. And the next.

Then the fifth of the nine. Nothing ran out of that one, and I reached a hand in and said, "What the hell—" The cat in it was dead.

I felt a little dizzy from bending over. I straightened up, and still felt dizzy. But I went to the sixth cage. It was harder to pull apart than the others, took me almost a minute. And the cat in it was dead, too. I looked toward the others, wondering if I was going to find all dead cats from there on; four live cats in a row and then the rest of the row of nine—

And quite suddenly I felt absurdly silly, as one feels in a dream sometimes, and wondered what I was doing here finding live cats and dead cats—and my mind was going around in dizzy circles, and when I stood up body swayed dizzily, too, and I couldn't get my balance.

Yes, I got it, then, and I tried to run. But too late. My feet wouldn't mind what I wanted them to do, and my knees went rubber and I didn't even feel pain from the impact of the ground hitting me as I went down.

As though from a great distance I heard a voice call, "Phil," and saw Ellen running toward me. I tried to motion her back and to call out to her to run away—but then things slipped away from under me, and I wasn't there any more. My last sensation before I completely lost consciousness was a tugging at my shoulders, as though someone was trying to drag me back to safety.

Then a steady light hurt my eyes, and I found I was lying on a wooden floor, so I knew that I had been unconscious for a while and was just coming to. There were voices.

Workus' voice and that of another man, an uninflected, monotonous voice. It was saying: "Yes, it is satisfactory. Reached to the cats in the first five cages; that's twenty-five feet. And only half a pound I put in the water pail. Think of half a ton!"

"But this guy and girl," I heard Workus saying. "It didn't kill them like it ought to. The girl's O.K. and Evans is coming to, already. So—"

A CAT WALKS

"Naturally, fool. I was on the way back and pulled them out in time. He couldn't have been in it more than three minutes, probably much less. And less than that for her, which is why she came out first. If it'd been five—"

Workus growled. "I still don't see why you didn't just leave them there that long."

"You see nothing. The bodies, of course. I want to keep on living here, even if an agent comes nosing around later. You are giving up your shop to go south, but I stay here. Nor would we want those bodies found dead anywhere else, dead of the gas."

I opened my eyes in time to see Workus nod assent. He said, "We shoot them, then? Sure, we've got their car. The bodies can be found in it, on the road miles from here."

"Yes," said the monotonous voice, and I turned my head to look toward the man who'd spoken.

I'd never seen him before, but he was worth looking at. He was tall and almost ridiculously thin, but his face was what drew my eyes. The skin was stretched so tightly over the bones that his head looked almost like a skull.

Pasty-white skin, and across the forehead was a vivid red scar that looked like a saber wound. It ran down into one empty eye socket uncovered by any patch or effort at concealment. The other eye turned upon me piercingly. "Our friend has come back," he said. "Peter, you take care of them."

The automatic was in Workus' hand. He said, "Here? But—"

"Here, yes," said the man with one eye. "They escaped once. We'll take no chances again." He grinned mirthlessly at me. "And if you hadn't escaped, you would have been freed—probably. But now, no."

I was able, for the first time since I'd seen him, to wrench my gaze away from his face enough to notice other things about him. First, that there was a gas mask slung about his neck, a type of mask which, when worn, covered all of the face except the eyes—which were huge circles of glass. He, then, had been the "faceless" man we'd seen on the path. He'd worn the mask, then.

Out of a corner of my eye, I saw Ellen sitting on a chair against the wall. The little gray cat was still in her arms, and her head was bent down over it, gently rubbing its fur with her chin. She smiled at me, a tremulous little smile that took real courage to produce. She said, "Well, Phil, we did find my cat."

Workus said, "Stand up, if you want, Evans. If you'd rather not take it lying down."

And I found, surprisingly, that I didn't want to take it lying down. Sounds funny that you'd feel that way when you're going to be shot, anyway. You'd think it doesn't matter how, but, somehow, it does.

I got up slowly, first to one knee, trying to take in as much of the room as I could in a quick glance around. Not that I expected to find a weapon in reach, or to see the United States marines coming through the doorway, or anything like that. But just in case.

If there was any way out of death for Ellen and myself, it would have to be tried within the next dozen seconds, and it wasn't going to cost anything to try. Maybe if I lunged for Workus before I got completely to my feet—

But it wouldn't have worked. He was six feet away; he'd be able to fire twice at point-blank range before I could get there. And he was ready for it.

There didn't seem to be anything that offered a chance of succeeding. There wasn't any furniture within reach. There were several chairs; the nearest was the one Ellen was sitting on. A kitchen table and a cupboard, but on the other side of the room. The back door was closed, and the one-eyed man stood beside it, as though ready to leave as soon as Workus had obeyed his orders.

A CAT WALKS 159

The light was from an electric bulb in the center of the ceiling, out of reach overhead. And there was a telephone—somehow it gave the impression of being newly installed—on the table. Also out of reach. Two windows, the bottom sash of one of them was raised.

Nothing within reach. Not a chance that I could see. Nothing remotely resembling a weapon. Except—

I started talking before I'd quite reached my feet. Workus had no reason to be in a hurry to shoot us; he'd probably let me finish whatever I started to say, as long as I didn't move closer to him.

"O.K., Workus," I said. "But we shouldn't have to die in vain, should we? After we went to all this trouble to get Miss Weyburn's cat, does it have to die, too?"

He was staring at me as though he thought I was crazy—and maybe I was crazy to think I could get away with this, but I figured that as long as I had him puzzled, he'd hold the trigger. I didn't, of course, wait for him to answer. I kept right on: "Look, if I'm giving up my life for a cat, you ought to be sport enough to let the cat go. And anyway, you can't shoot Miss Weyburn while she's holding—" She wasn't holding the cat any more, though, because I'd just turned around and taken it from her, and I was turning with it in my hands toward the open window.

As though I were going to drop the cat out the window; but I didn't. I'd timed my turn and synchronized the motion of my arms for the throw, and even before the man with one eye yelled, "Hey!" and the automatic in Workus' hands went off, the cat was sailing through the air at Workus' face.

He pulled the trigger all right, but he ducked while he was doing it, and the bullet missed me by inches. It's not easy to shoot straight when there's a cat hurtling at one's face, its claws out ready to grab the first available object to stop its flight.

And I was going in toward Workus behind the cat, and almost as fast. Swinging a roundhouse right as I went; aiming at his stomach as the biggest and hardest to miss target for a blow I couldn't take time to aim carefully.

The cat caught its claws in the shoulder of his coat and then jumped on down to the floor just as my fist made connections. The blow had all my weight and the force of my run behind it. He didn't pull the trigger a second time, and I heard the automatic clatter to the floor as he started to fall.

I didn't take time to go after that gun; I whirled toward the man standing by the door and I was starting toward him almost before I'd finished my blow at Workus.

The one-eyed man was bringing a pistol—which had been, apparently, in his hip pocket—around and up. But things had happened too fast, and he hadn't reached for it soon enough. Or maybe he'd fumbled in getting it out of his pocket. Anyway, I got there before he could lift and aim it. I didn't take time to swing at him; I simply ran smack into him with a straight arm that caught him full in the face and smacked his head against the door behind him so hard that I thought, from the sound of it, that I'd killed him.

I whirled back to see if Workus was going for the gun he'd dropped, but he was sitting on the floor, doubled up and groaning in pain, and Ellen had the gun.

I said, "Atta girl," and then picked up the other gun and put it in my pocket and went for the phone. I called Hank Granville's home number and got a sleepily grunted "hello" after a minute or two.

"Hank," I said, "this is Phil. Say, about that Dean-laboratory burglary and murder. Was the secrecy because they'd been working on an odorless lethal gas? Something in solid form that you drop in water like carbide, and it—"

"Hey!" Hank sounded suddenly very wide awake. "Phil, for God's sake where'd you find that out? It's supposed to be—"

"Yeah," I cut in. "Secret. But a guy by the name of Workus

A CAT WALKS

who had a front as a pet-shop owner, and another guy, got it. Dunno whether they got it to peddle to a foreign power, or what, but they weren't sure they had the right stuff and they wanted to test just how good it was. That's what they wanted cats for; to see how far a given quantity of it would spread."

"The hell! Phil, this is big! If you're right— Where the devil are you?"

"I don't know," I told him. "Somewhere in the country. But I got both guys here, and everything's under control. I'll leave this receiver off the hook and you can get the call traced and come out with the Maria. So long."

And without waiting for him to answer, I put the receiver down on the table and crossed over to Ellen. She'd just picked up the little gray cat, which looked a bit ruffled, but unhurt. She was soothing and petting it and talking baby talk to it.

I said, "Gosh, I'm sorry I had to throw it, but— Maybe I can make friends with it again."

And I reached out a doubtful hand, not knowing whether I'd get clawed or not. But I wasn't. Ellen smiled at me, and the cat began to purr. And I put my arms around Ellen and she had to put the cat down because it was in the way. I hoped it would be a long time before the police got there and I felt like purring myself.

THE MISSING ACTOR

"Hunter and Hunter," I told the telephone, and it asked me if this was one of the Mr. Hunters speaking and I said yes, I was Ed Hunter.

And I was, and still am. Hunter & Hunter is a two-man detective agency operated on State Street on the Near North Side of Chicago. My Uncle Am for Ambrose is shortish, fattish, and smartish; he'd been an operative for a private detective agency once back when and then had become a carney. We got together after my father's death ten years ago when I was eighteen, spent a couple of seasons together with a carnival, and then got jobs as operatives for the Starlock Agency in Chicago, and after a few years of that started our own detective agency, just the two of us. It's still a peanut operation, but we like peanuts. We get along with each other and most of the world, and we make a living.

"Floyd Nielson," the phone said. "Like you to do a job for me. Be there if I come around now?"

"One of us will be here," I said, "and probably both. But could you tell me what kind of a job it is? If it's some sort of work we can't or don't handle, I can save you the trip."

"Missing person. My son Albee. Want you to find him."

"Have you tried the police?"

"Sure. Missing Persons. Guy named Chudakoff. Lieutenant, I think. Said he'd done all he could, unless there's new information. Said if I wanted more done, I should get a private agency. Recommended yours."

Sounded okay, I thought, getting into his laconic way of talking. Every once in a while some friend of ours in the department tosses something our way, and in that case it's bound to be on the up and up. Only honest people go to the cops first and then sometimes turn out to want more help than the cops can give them.

"How soon will you be here, Mr. Nielson?" I asked.

"Hour. Maybe less. I'm at the Ideal Hotel on South State. You're on North State. Must be a bus that takes me through the Loop. Probably faster'n getting a taxi."

I told him the number of the bus, where to catch it, and where to get off. He thanked me and hung up.

I put down the phone and was just about to pick it up again to call Tom Chudakoff to see what I could learn about the case in advance; then I looked at my watch and realized Uncle Am was already a few minutes overdue back from lunch and decided to wait and let him listen in on the call. Either or both of us might be working on the case.

He came in a minute later and I told him about the call from Nielson, what there'd been of it, and suggested he listen in on my call to Lieutenant Chudakoff. He said okay and went into his office, the inner one, and picked up his phone while I was dialing.

I got Chudakoff right away and told him what we wanted.

"Nielson, sure," he said. "He's been heckling me and I got him out of my hair by sending him to you. If you make any money out of him, you owe me a dinner."

"Okay," I said. "But he's on his way here now, and what can you tell us in advance?"

THE MISSING ACTOR

"That there's no problem. His son owed a bookie eight hundred bucks and took a powder. It's as mysterious as all that."

"If his father's solvent enough to hire detective work, wasn't he solvent enough to stand a bite to pay the bookie?"

"Oh, he gave the money to Albee all right. But it never got to the bookie. Albee thought it was better used as a fresh stake, I'd guess. He'd just lost his job, so what did he have to lose glomming onto the money himself."

"Tell me something about him. Albee, I mean."

"Well, he had a fairly good job in a bookstore, and a padded pad, was fairly solvent and played ponies on the cuff with a bookie named Red Kogan. Know him?"

"Heard of him," I said.

"Well, Albee booked with him and always paid up when he lost until, all of a sudden a little over a week ago, Kogan realized Albee was into him for eight hundred. One of his boys drops in at Albee's pad and doesn't connect. He goes around to the bookstore and learns Albee's been fired from his job. So what's mysterious?"

"A padded pad, for one thing. What is one?"

"Albee was a part-time hipster. He was square eight hours a day—or whatever—at the bookstore, hip in his spare time. Look over his pad and you'll see what I mean."

"When was he last seen, Tom?"

"Week ago last Saturday night, July sixth. He borrowed car keys from a friend of his, Jerry Score, on Saturday morning—that's the day after he was fired from the bookstore. Gave 'em back late evening. If any of his friends, or anybody else, has seen him since, they're not talking."

"Sure. Said he was in a jam and wanted to see his old man—that's your client—to raise some scratch. Floyd Nielson was a truck farmer near Kenosha, Wisconsin—"

"What do you mean, was?" I cut in. "Isn't he now?"

"Sold his truck farm ten days ago, getting ready to blow this part of the country. He's in Chicago, trying to see his son for one last time first."

"But he saw him only nine days ago."

"Yeah. It's not so much that, or rather, I shouldn't have put it that way. It's that he wants to be sure Albee is okay before he takes off.

"And he thinks he's sure Albee wouldn't run off, just to duck an eight hundred dollar debt—at least not when he had the eight hundred in hand. Says Albee likes Chicago and has a lot of friends here, that he wouldn't leave just because of that. Maybe he's got a point, I wouldn't know, but hell, there's no evidence of foul play or anything *but* a run-out, and we can't spend any more of taxpayers' money on it. I can keep it open on the books, and that's all, from here on in. That is, unless something new turns up. If you boys take the case and can turn up something, like maybe a motive for somebody dusting him off, we'll work on it again."

"Isn't his running out on the bookie a motive?"

"Ed, this isn't the old days. Bookies don't have people killed for peanuts like that. Besides, Kogan's not that kind of guy. He might lean on Albee a little, but that's all. Probably *did* lean on him, which is what scared the guy. If Albee's stayed, he'd have turned over the money—it's just that he figured he'd rather use it as a stake for a fresh start somewhere else, and he had to do it one way or the other. Take my word for it."

"Makes sense, Tom," I said. "But if it's that cut and dried, aren't we just taking money away from a poor old man to take the case at all?"

"He's not that poor. Frugal, yes; don't try to bite him too hard."

He was just kidding, so I didn't answer that. He and our other cop friends know that we don't bomb our clients. Which is why they send business our way once in a while.

"Find out anything else interesting about Albee?" I asked.

THE MISSING ACTOR

"Well, he had a hell of a cute little colored sweetie-pie. These beat boys seem to go for that."

"First," I said, "you say he's hip, now he's beat. Which is he?"

"Is there a difference?"

I said, "Norman Mailer seems to think so."

"Who is Norman Mailer?"

"That," I said, "is a good question. But back to this girl. What color is she? Green? Orange? Or what?"

"Ed, she's Hershey-bar colored. But listen, why pry this stuff out of me piecemeal? I've got the file handy, so why don't I give you names and addresses of people we talked to—there aren't many—and what they told us. Then maybe you'll let me get back to work and quit yakking."

I told him that would be fine and I pulled over a pad of foolscap and made notes, and when I finished, Uncle Am and I knew as much as the police did. About the disappearance of Albee Nielson, anyway. I thanked Chudakoff and hung up.

Uncle Am came out of the inner office and sat down across from my desk in the outer one. "Well, kid," he asked, "how does it hit you?"

I shrugged. "Looks like Albee just took a powder, all right. But if Nielson wants to spend a little before he's convinced, who are we to talk him out of it?"

"Nobody. Anyway, we'll see what he's got to say."

It wasn't long before we heard what he had to say. Nielson looked anywhere in his fifties. Grizzled graying hair and a beard to match, steel-rimmed glasses, and the red skin and redder neck of a man who's worked outdoors all his life, even under a relatively mild Wisconsin sun.

"Damn cops," he said. "That Chudakoff. Wouldn't believe me. *Told* him Albee wouldn't run away. Not for eight hundred dollars, and when he had it."

I asked, "How did you and Albee get along, Mr. Nielson? In general, and the day he came to you for the money?"

"General, fair. Oh, we didn't see eye-to-eye on a lot of things. Crazy ideas, he had. Left me alone the minute he got through high school, came to Chicago. But we kept in touch. Letter once in a while. And he dropped up once in a while, sometimes just overnight, sometimes a whole weekend. Usually when he could borrow a car."

"You ever visit him here?"

"Once-twice a year, if I had business in Chicago. Not overnight, 'less I had business that kept me. Then I stayed at a hotel, though. Didn't think much of that—what he called a pad, of his."

"What about Albee's mother? And any brothers or sisters he was close to?"

"No brothers or sisters. Mother died when he was twelve. What's *she* got to do with it?"

"We're just trying to get the whole picture, Mr. Nielson," I said. "And Albee and you lived alone till he was graduated from high school and he came to Chicago?"

He nodded, and I asked, "How long ago was that?"

" 'Leven-twelve years. Albee's thirty now."

"Did he ever borrow money from you during that time?"

"Small amounts a few times. If he was out of work a while or something. But always paid it back, when he got a job. That was back when. Ain't borrowed since, till now, from the time he got that bookstore job. That paid pretty good."

"So you didn't worry about his paying back the current eight hundred?"

"Oh, it'd of taken him a time to do it, but he would of. Especially as he'd learned his lesson—I think—and was through with gambling." He stopped long enough to light a pipe he'd been tamping down. "Oh, I bawled hell out of him before I give it to him. That kind of gambling, I mean. Not that I'm agin gambling in reason. Used to go into Kenosha most every Saturday night myself for a little poker. But stakes I could afford. It was going

THE MISSING ACTOR 169

in *debt* gambling that I laid Albee out for. Laid him out plenty, 'fore I give him the money."

"But you didn't actually quarrel?"

"Some, at first. But we got over it and he stayed for supper, and we talked about my plans, now I'm partially retiring."

"What do you mean by partly retiring, Mr. Nielson?" Uncle Am cut in with that; I'd been wondering whether to ask it or skip it.

"Place near Kenosha's a little too much for me to handle any more. By myself, that is, and I don't like hired hands. Always quit on you when you're in a jam.

"So I'd decided — if I could get my price, and I did, near enough — to sell it and get a smaller truck farm. One I could handle by myself, even when I get some older'n I am now. Maybe give me time to set in the sun an hour or two a day, not work twelve, sometimes more, hours a day like I been. *And* in a milder climate.

"That's mostly what me and Albee talked about. I'd thought Florida. Albee said California climate'd be better for me, dryer."

"Have you made up your mind now which?"

"Yes-no. Made up my mind to take a look at California. *Saw* Florida once. If I like California better, and find what I want, I'll stay."

"And since this conversation with Albee a week ago Saturday, you haven't heard from him? Not even a letter?"

"Nope. No reason for him to write. Told him I'd be passing through Chicago in a few days on my way either to Florida or California, hadn't made up my mind for sure which then, and that I'd look him up to say so long. That was the last thing between us."

"And this would have been about eight o'clock Saturday evening, which would have got him back to Chicago about ten."

"It's about two hours' drive, yes. And I left Monday. Didn't take me long to pack up as I thought. Been here since, a week today. Want to find Albee, or what happened to him — or something — before I take off. No hurry in my getting to California, but I'm wasting time here and I don't like Chicago. Kill time seeing a lot of movies, but that's about all I can do. That Chudakoff, he thinks Albee run off. I still don't. He says if I want more looking, try you. Here I am."

"And if we have no better luck than the police," I asked, "or if we decide they're right in deciding your son left town voluntarily, how long do you intend to stay in Chicago?"

Nielson burst into a sudden cackle of laughter that startled me. Up to now he hadn't cracked a smile. "What you're asking is how much I want to spend. Let's take it from the other end. How much do you charge?"

I glanced at Uncle Am so he'd know to take over; when we're both around I always let him do the talking on money.

"Seventy-five a day," he said. "And expenses. I suggest you give us a retainer of two hundred; that'll cover two days and expenses. That'll be long enough for us to give you at least a preliminary report. And there shouldn't be many expenses, so if you decide to call it off at the end of two days you'll probably have a rebate coming."

Nielson frowned. "Seventy-five a day for both of you to work on it or for one?"

I let Uncle Am tell him it was for one of us, and argue it from there. He finally came down to sixty a day, saying it was our absolute minimum rate — which it is, for private clients. We charge less only to insurance companies, skip-trace outfits, and others who give us recurrent trade. And Uncle Am finally settled for a retainer of one-fifty, which would allow thirty for expenses.

Nielson counted it out in twenties and a ten. Then he had another thought and wanted to know if today would count for a day, since it was already two in the afternoon. Uncle Am assured

THE MISSING ACTOR

him it wouldn't, unless whichever of us worked on it worked late enough into the evening to make it a full day.

I'd thought of another question meanwhile. "Mr. Nielson, when Albee borrowed the money from you, did he tell you he'd lost his job at the bookstore?"

He gave that cackle-laugh again. "No, he didn't. I didn't find out that till I phoned the store to see if I could get him at work. Albee's smart, figured I'd be less likely to lend him money if I knew he was out of work. Guess I would of anyway—he's never been out of a job long—but he didn't know that and I don't blame him for playing safe. Told me he wasn't working that Saturday 'cause the store was closed for three days, Friday through Sunday, for remodeling."

"One other thing, did you give him cash or a check? If it was a check we'll know something when we find out where it clears from. He couldn't have cashed a check that size late Saturday night or on a Sunday."

"It was cash. I'd closed out my bank account, had quite a bit of cash, cashier's check for the rest. Still got enough I won't have to use that cashier's check till I'm ready to buy another truck farm."

He stood up to go and we both walked to the door with him. Uncle Am asked something I should have thought of. "Mr. Nielson, if he still *is* in Chicago and we find him, what do we tell him? Just to get in touch with you at the Ideal Hotel?"

"You can make it stronger'n that. Tell him to get in touch with me or else. I never made a will, see, so being my only living blood relative, he's still my heir. But it don't have to stay that way. I can make a will in California and cut him off. Cost him a lot more than eight hundred dollars, someday."

He reached for the doorknob but Uncle Am's question and its answer had made me think of something. I said, "Just a minute, Mr. Nielson. Has this possibility occurred to you? That he did blow town while he had that eight hundred as a stake, rather than pay it to a bookie just to stay here, but that he intends to write to you as soon as he's got another job somewhere and can start paying off what he owes you?"

"Yep, that's possible. Sure I thought of it."

"This is not my business, Mr. Nielson, but if that does happen, would you still make a will to disinherit him?"

"Make up my mind if and when it happens. Maybe according to what he says when he writes, and if he really does start paying back. Right now I'm mad at him if that's what happened — if he did that without letting me know so I wouldn't waste time and money trying to find him here. But I could get over my mad, I guess."

"If you don't know just where you're going in California, how are you having your mail forwarded?"

"Fellow bought from me's going to hold it for me till I write him. But no letter's come yet could be from Albee. I phoned last night to make sure. Just a couple bills and circulars. No personal letters like could be from Albee even if he changed his name. I thought of that, son. May be a farmer, but I ain't dumb."

"That I see," I said. "And you'll probably phone Kenosha once more the last thing before you start driving west?"

"Right, except for the driving. Sold my pickup truck with the farm. Buy another in California. Be a hell of a long drive, rather go by train."

"Do you want written reports?" I asked him.

"Don't see what good they'd do. Just phone me at the hotel what you find out. If I see any more movies before I go, I'll do it by day, stay there evenings so you can call me. Or Albee can, if you find him."

That seemed to cover everything anybody could think of so we let him leave. Uncle Am strolled into his inner office and I strolled after him.

THE MISSING ACTOR 173

"What do you think, Uncle Am?" I asked.

He shrugged. "That Albee took a powder. I think his papa thinks so too, but if he wants to let us spend a couple of days making a final try, more power to him. He's a stubborn old coot."

"Uh-huh," I said. "Well, I guess it's my turn to work on it. You put in four days' work last week and I got in only two. This'll even it up."

"Okay, kid. Going to take the car?"

I shook my head. "Most of the places are pretty near here. I'll do it faster on foot or an occasional taxi hop than having to find places to park."

He yawned and took a deck of cards out of his desk to play some solitaire. "Okay. I'll be here till five. Think you'll work this evening, or call it half a day today?"

"I might as well work through," I said. "So don't figure on dinner with me and look for me when you see me."

I went back to my desk and took the paper I'd taken the notes on during my conversation with Chudakoff. And said so long to Uncle Am and left.

I decided to go to the bookstore first. It might close at five, and the other addresses I had were personal ones and I'd probably stand a better chance of finding the people I wanted to talk to by evening than by day.

It was the Prentice Bookstore on Michigan Avenue. I'd never been inside it, but I knew where it was. It took me about twenty minutes to walk there.

There weren't any customers at the moment. A clerk up front, a girl, told me Mr. Heiden, the proprietor, was in his office at the back. I went back, found him studying some publishers' catalogs, introduced myself and showed him identification.

"You let Albee Nielson go on Friday, the fifth?"

"Yes. And haven't seen him. I told everything I knew to the detective — the *city* detective — that came here last week. Who you working for? The man he owed money to?"

"For Albee's father," I said. "He's worried about his son's disappearance. For his sake, do you mind answering a few more questions?"

He gave me a grudging "What are they?" and put down the catalog he'd been looking at.

"Why did you fire Albee?"

"I'm afraid that that's one I *won't* answer."

"Had you given him notice?"

"No."

"Then doesn't that pretty well answer the other question? You must have found that he was dipping in the till, or knocking down some way or other. But decided not to prosecute, and now it'd be too late, and it'd be slander if you said that about him."

He give me a smile, but a pretty thin one. "That wasn't a question, Mr. Hunter. I can't control what conclusions you may choose to draw."

"Would you give him a recommendation for another job?"

"No, I wouldn't. But I would refuse to give my reasons for not giving one."

"That would be your privilege," I admitted. And since I wasn't getting anywhere on that tract, I tried another. "Do you know anything about Albee's life outside the job? Names of any of his friends, anything at all about him personally?"

"Not a thing, I'm afraid. Except his home address and telephone number, and of course you already have those. Before he started here I checked a couple of references he gave me, but I'm afraid I've forgotten now what they were except that they checked out all right. That was almost five years ago."

"Do you remember what kind of jobs they were?"

"One was taking want-ads for a newspaper, but I forget which newspaper. The other was clerking in a hardware store—but I don't remember now even in what part of town it was. And as for friends of his, no. He must have, or have had, some, but none

THE MISSING ACTOR

of them ever came here to see him. Almost as though he told them not to, as though he deliberately wanted to keep his business life and his social life completely separated. I've never known even what *kind* of friends he had. And he never talked about himself."

He was being friendly now and cooperating, once we'd skirted the subject of why he'd fired Albee. But his very refusal to answer that question, I thought, pretty well did answer it.

So I did the only thing I could do, gave him a business card and asked him to call us if he did happen to think of anything at all that might be the slightest help in our finding Albee for his father. He promised to do that, and maybe he even meant it.

On my way out, I saw the girl clerk was still or again free and asked her if she'd known Albee Nielson. The name registered, but only from seeing it on sales slips and employment records. She'd worked there only a week and had been taken on because Nielson, as she thought, had quit the job.

So I went out into the hot July sunlight again. Next was Albee's pad, and his landlady. On a short street called Seneca, near the lake. Only a ten minute walk this time; he'd picked a place conveniently near to where he had worked. Handy to the beach, too, if he swam or sun-bathed.

It was an old stone front, three stories, that had probably been a one-family residence in its day but had now been divided into a dozen rooms. That's how many mailboxes there were and there was a buzzer button under each. Nielson was the name on No. 9, and I pushed the buzzer button under it. Even took hold of the doorknob in case an answering buzz should indicate that the lock was being temporarily released. But I got just what I expected to get, no answering buzz. Well, that was good in one way; if Albee had been home and had let me come up to see him, we'd have had to give Floyd Nielson most of his hundred and fifty bucks. We couldn't have charged more than half a day's time, and expenses so far had run to zero.

I went back and looked through the glass of Nielson's mailbox. There was something in it that looked like it was a bill, but I couldn't read the return address. The lock was one of those simple little ones that open with a tiny flat key; if I'd thought to bring our picklock along I could have had it open in thirty seconds, but one can't think of everything.

I looked over the other mailboxes for a Mrs. Radcliffe; Chudakoff had said she was the landlady. Sure enough, it was No. 1, and had "Landlady" written under the name in the slot. I pushed her button and put my hand on the knob of the door; this time it buzzed and released itself and I went on through.

Mrs. Radcliffe had the door of No. 1 opened and was waiting for me in the doorway. She was about fifty and was small and wiry. Chicago rooming house landladies come in all sizes but most of them have two things in common, hard eyes and a tough look. Mrs. Radcliffe wasn't one of the exceptions, and I was sure, too, that she hadn't named herself after a college she'd been graduated from.

I gave her a business card and the song and dance about Albee's poor old father being worried about him, but it didn't soften her eyes any. Finally I got to questions.

"When did you last see Albee, Mrs. Radcliffe?"

"Don't remember exactly, but it was over a week ago. Then, just seeing him come in or go out. Last time I talked to him was on the first. Paid me a month's rent then; it's still his place till the end of the month, whether he comes back to it or not."

"Have you been in it, since then?"

"No. I rent 'em as is, and people do their own cleaning. I don't go in, till after they've left, to get it cleaned up for the next tenant."

"Are they rented furnished or unfurnished?"

"Unfurnished, except for stove and refrigerator; there's a kitchenette in each for them who want to do light housekeeping. And each one has its own bathroom. Couples live in a few of 'em, but they're fine for one person."

THE MISSING ACTOR 177

"Would you mind letting me look inside Albee's?"

"Yes. It's his till his rent's up."

"But you let Lieutenant Chudakoff go up and look around. We're working the same side of the fence. In fact, he's a friend of mine."

"But he's a real cop and you're not. Bring him with you and I'll let you go up with him."

I sighed. "He's a busy man, Mrs. Radcliffe. If I get him to write you a letter, on police stationery, asking you to let me borrow a key, will that do?"

"Guess so. Or even if he tells me over the phone."

I wondered how I'd been so stupid as not to think of that short cut. The phone, I'd already noticed, was a pay one, on the wall behind me. I got a dime out of my pocket and started for it.

But she said, "Wait a minute. How do I know you'd dial the right number? You could call any number and have somebody there to say his name is Chudakoff. He gave me his card. *I'll* dial it." Apparently she'd put the card on a stand right beside the door; she was able to get it without leaving the doorway. She held out a hand. "I'll use your dime, though."

While she dialed, I grinned to myself at how suspicious she was—and how right. I *could* have set it up with Uncle Am to have answered "Missing Persons. Chudakoff speaking."

She finished dialing and I heard her say, "Mr. Chudakoff please." She listened a few seconds and then hung up.

"He's out of the office, won't be back till tomorrow morning. You can try again then, if you've got another dime."

I sighed and decided to give up till tomorrow. Well, at least that's run the investigation into a second day.

I said, "All right, I'll be back then. Mrs. Radcliffe, do you know any of Albee's friends?"

"A few by sight, none by name. And, like I told Mr. Chudakoff, I wouldn't have an idea where he might of gone to, if he's really gone. Unless to see his father near Kenosha, and you say it's him that's looking for Albee."

I tried a new tack, not that I expected it to get me anywhere. "Has Albee been a good tenant?"

"Except a couple of things. Played his phonograph too loud a time or two and others on the third floor complained and I told him about it. And something I don't hold with personally— he's brought a girl here. But that's his business, the way I look at it."

Well, I didn't pursue that. I had the girl's name on my list. I thanked Mrs. Radcliffe, and left. I'd be back tomorrow, I decided, but first I'd make sure Chudakoff would be in his office ready for the call.

Next on my list was a Jerry Score, identified by Chudakoff as Albee's closest friend. Chudakoff hadn't got anything helpful out of him, but I could try. Especially as he lived only two blocks away, on Walton Place.

It turned out to be a rooming house building pretty much like the one in which Albee had his pad, except with four stories and more rooms. Again I got silence in answer to buzzing the room, and again I tried a landlady, whose name turned out to be Mrs. Proust, although this one labeled herself "Proprietor." This one was big, fat and sloppy, and the heat was getting her down.

But she gave me the score on Jerry Score. He wouldn't be home; he was out of town for the day. She didn't know where, but he'd said he'd be back tomorrow. And she was sure he would be, because he was playing the second lead in a play for the Near Northers, a little theater group, and was having to rehearse almost every afternoon and evening. She told me where they were rehearsing and would be playing, an old theater on Clark Street that had once been a burlesque house and was now used only by little theater groups. And yes, she was sure he'd be there tomorrow afternoon because that was the last rehearsal before the dress rehearsal.

THE MISSING ACTOR 179

She was panting by then and invited me in for a cold lemonade, probably because she wanted one herself, and the lemonade tasted good and she was bottled up with talk. Yes, she knew Jerry pretty well, he'd been with her for years. His job? He was a door-to-door canvasser, vacuum cleaners, and did pretty well at it. He liked that kind of work because he could set his own hours and that let him go in for amateur theatricals. He'd wanted to be a pro and had once made a try at Hollywood, but had given up and came back. He gave her duckets and she'd seen him act and thought he was pretty good. She was show people herself; back when, she'd been a pony in a chorus line, with a traveling troupe that had once played the very theater Jerry was now acting in.

Yes, she knew Albee Nielson. Not real well, but she'd met him a few times, and had seen him act too. Yes, he'd been with the Near Northers, but not in the current play, and Jerry had told her, she thought about a week ago, that Albee had left town.

In case she might be holding something back—although she sure didn't sound as though she was—I trotted out the poor old father bit for her, telling her that finding Albee for his father was the reason I wanted to see Jerry Score.

It didn't help, but she'd have helped if she could. Jerry hadn't told her where Albee had gone, and she didn't think Jerry knew. I believed her and was convinced she couldn't tell me more than she had about Albee; that is, anything that would be helpful in finding him.

Not that she wasn't willing to keep on talking—about anything at all. I had to make my escape or soon she'd have been bringing out her press clippings and theatrical photos of two dozen years ago. But I liked her and promised to come back some time, and meant it.

It was five o'clock. The next name on my list was Honey Howard, Albee's inamorata. She lived a taxi jump away, on Schiller Street a couple blocks west of Clark Street. But the

Graydon Theater, the ex-burlesque house that was now used only by little theater groups like and including the Near Northers, was on Clark just a block or two from Schiller, so I decided to take a taxi there, and walk to Honey's from the theater. Probably I'd find no one at the theater, but if they'd had an afternoon rehearsal without Jerry Score and it had run late, someone might still be there.

I used the phone in the hallway near Mrs. Proust's door to call a cab and waited for it outside. Surprisingly, for such a rush hour, it came fairly quickly, and it was only five-thirty when I disembarked in front of the Graydon.

I walked through the lobby, its walls ornate with plaster nymphs and satyrs, and tried the doors but found them locked. But there'd be a stage entrance around off the alley and I headed for it, neared it just in time to see a distinguished-looking elderly gentleman turn a key in the lock of the door and come toward me. I begged his pardon and asked if he was connected with the Near Northers.

He smiled. "You might almost say I *am* the Near Northers, young man. I started the group four years ago and have been manager ever since and director of every alternate play we've put on since. I'm directing the current one. What can I do for you?"

I introduced myself and told him I was interested in Albee Nielson, and why.

He told me that he didn't know a lot about Albee personally, but he'd be glad to tell me what he did know. Where should we talk? We could go back into the theater, or there was a quiet bar a block down the street if I cared to have a drink with him.

It was half past five and I decided on the drink. I'd be eating soon, maybe before I looked up Honey Howard if my talk with the little theater group's manager-director ran very long.

He introduced himself, while we walked, as Carey Evers. The name sounded vaguely familiar to me, and it occurred to me that his face was slightly familiar too. I asked him if I'd ever seen him before, possibly on television or in movies.

Quite probably, he told me, if I ever watched old movies on late-late shows. He'd started in them about the time they were making the transition from silents to talkies. He'd played bit parts and character roles. Never important parts, never starred, but he'd been in a hundred and sixty-four movies. A great many of them were B's, most of them in fact, but they were still being rerun on television. He'd never tried to make the transition to television per se. He'd retired seven years ago.

We were in the bar, sitting in a booth over drinks, by that time. He stopped talking, waiting for me to start asking my questions about Albee, but instead I asked him how much time he had.

He glanced at his watch. "An hour or so. Dinner date at seven, but it's near here; I won't have to leave until a quarter of."

"Good," I said. "Then keep on about yourself for at least a few more minutes. How you came to Chicago after you retired, and how you started the Near Northers."

He'd bought a place in Malibu when he'd retired, he told me, but he'd never liked California. "Hated the place, in fact. And I'd been born and raised in Chicago—broke into show business here, night club work—and didn't go to Hollywood till I was almost thirty. And I found myself homesick for Chicago after I had nothing to do out there, so I sold the Malibu place within a year and came back. Bought a house on Lake Shore Drive, but near the Near North Side, my old haunt.

"And after a while, found myself bored with nothing to do, and homesick for show biz again, and discovered little theater. Worked with two other groups, and then started my own. It's wonderful. I work fourteen hours a day, except when I rest between plays, and love it."

He grinned wryly. "And these kids love me—if only because

I'm angel as well as manager-director." He explained that almost all little theater groups operated at a deficit, especially if they wanted to do good work and put on good plays, the public be damned, and still keep ticket prices low enough so they'd have a good audience to play to.

Carey Evers had retired not rich but with a lot more money then he'd be able to use during the rest of his life, and could think of no better way to spend it, and his time; as long as he remained strong and healthy enough, he'd keep on doing what he was doing. He loved it.

In answer to a question, he told me that no, the actors didn't make any money out of it; they worked for the love of acting, for the fun of it, and some of them with the hope of learning enough to become professionals someday. And two kids out of the original group he'd started with four years ago were now doing bit parts in television, another was now an announcer on a Chicago television station.

"Do you ever lend any of them money?" I asked, and then cut in before he could answer. "Wait. That's none of my business, but this is: Did Albee Nielson ever borrow or try to borrow money from you?"

He nodded. "About three weeks ago, he came to me and tried to borrow five hundred. I turned him down. In the first place, I never lend money in amounts like that and in the second, I didn't believe his story, that it was for an operation for his father. I knew enough about him to know that his father was solvent, and I knew Albee was working steady—he was then—but playing the horses. I put two and two together.

"And from what I've learned since, my addition was correct. In fact, in the week or so after that he apparently ran a few hundred more in the hole trying to get out."

"Was that the last time you saw him?"

He nodded. "That was when we were casting the current play

THE MISSING ACTOR

and I asked him if he wanted to try out for a part. He didn't. It was too bad; he's a pretty good actor. I'd say almost but not quite professional, or potentially professional, caliber. He had the lead role in two plays we've put on, strong supporting parts in several others."

"What else do you know about him? Especially his personal life?"

He talked a while, but I didn't know any more when he'd told me all he could than I had when he'd started. Yes, Jerry Score was his closest friend, Honey Howard was his girl. And other things I'd already learned.

I asked him if he knew where Jerry Score was today. It turned out in Hammond, Indiana, for the funeral of an uncle. "Went there a little early to have some time with his family. The funeral's tomorrow morning, and Jerry will rush right back for afternoon rehearsal. He'll probably come right from the train, so you'll do better finding him at the Graydon than trying his room. We start rehearsal at one-thirty."

"Will I be able to talk to him during rehearsal, or should I wait till after?"

"During. He's not on stage *all* the time. Ed, would you like a ducket or two for the show, Thursday evening? Or any night through Sunday, for that matter; we run four days."

I told him I'd manage to make it one of the four but would just as soon kick through with a paid admission to help the cause.

Then he asked me about me, and about being a private detective, and *I* got to talking. And was still going strong when suddenly I saw that it was ten of seven and reminded him about his appointment. He lost another half minute giving me a fight over the check — it was only for two drinks apiece — then gave up and ran.

I paid the check and left more slowly because I was trying to decide whether to call on Honey Howard first, or after eating.

I was beginning to get pretty hungry, but duty won when I realized I'd have a better chance of finding her in now than maybe an hour later when she could have left for the evening.

It was another stone front; it was my day for stone fronts. One mailbox had two names on it, Wilcox and Howard, and the number six. But there was no bell button and the door wasn't locked so I went in and started checking room numbers, found Number Six on the second floor, and knocked.

A tall, quite beautiful colored girl opened the door. But very light colored—far from Hershey-bar—so I felt sure she would be the Wilcox of the two names on the mailbox, Honey Howard's roommate. I asked her if Miss Howard was there. She said yes, and then stepped back. "Honey, someone to see *you.*"

And Honey appeared at the doorway instead. Hershey-bar, yes, but petite and *very* beautiful, much more so than her tall, light roommate.

I gave her my best smile and went into my spiel.

"You might as well come in, Mr. Hunter," she said, stepping back. I followed her into a nicely furnished, bright and cheerful double room pretty much like the one Uncle Am and I live in on Huron Street.

"I'm willing to help if I can, Mr. Hunter," she said, "but I hope this won't take very long. Lissa and I were just about to go out to eat."

It was the perfect opening. I said, "I'm ravenously hungry myself, Miss Howard. May I invite both of you to have dinner with me? Then we can talk while we eat, and it won't take up any of anybody's time." I grinned at her. "And we'll all eat for free because I can put it on my client's expense account."

She gave a quick glance at her roommate and apparently got an affirmative because she turned back and returned my grin. "All right, especially if it's on Mr. Nielson. After the way Albee ran out on me without even telling me he was going, guess the Nielsons owe me at least a dinner. Let's go."

THE MISSING ACTOR

And we went, although first I instigated a conversation as to where they wanted to go so we could phone for a cab. But the place they wanted to go, I had in fact been intending to go anyway, was only two blocks south on Clark Street, only a few blocks away and they'd rather walk.

It turned out to be a fairly nice restaurant, called *Robair's*. The proprietor knew the girls and came over to our table while we were having cocktails and I was introduced to him and he grinned and admitted that his name was really Robert but that he knew how the name was pronounced in French and thought it a little swankier to spell it that way. He was colored and so were the waitresses and most of the clientele, but I was far from being the only ofay in the place.

When I started asking questions, Honey Howard answered them freely, or seemed to. Of course I didn't ask anything about her personal relationships with him; that was none of my business.

She'd last seen him Thursday evening, two evenings before the time he'd been seen last. No, he hadn't said anything about going away anywhere, not even about a possibility of his going up to Kenosha to see his father. Nor anything about his job or a possibility of his losing it. But he had been moody and depressed, and had admitted he owed a bundle to his bookie and was worried about it. She'd told him she had fifty bucks saved up and wanted to know if lending him that would help. He'd thanked her but said it would not, that it was a hell of a lot more than that.

No, she hadn't heard from him since. And she made that convincing by admitting she was a bit hurt about it. Quite a bit, in fact. The least he could have done would have been to telephone her to say goodbye and he hadn't even done that.

No, she had no idea where he might have gone, except that it would have been another big city—like New York or Los Angeles or San Francisco. He hated small towns. Or maybe

Paris—Paris was the only specific place he'd ever talked about *wanting* to go to.

I considered that for a moment because it was the only specific place that had been mentioned thus far as a place he'd like to go. I asked Honey—we were Honey and Lissa and Ed by now— whether he spoke French. He didn't, and I pretty well ruled Paris out. With only eight hundred bucks and little chance of getting a job there, it would be a silly place for him to go, however glamorous it might look to him. Besides, with a sudden change of identity that left him no provable antecedents, he'd have hell's own time getting a passport.

No, I wasn't going to learn anything helpful from Honey. Jerry Score, tomorrow, would be my last hope. And a slender one.

We'd finished eating by then and I suggested a brandy to top the dinner off. Honey agreed, but Lissa said she had to leave; she worked as hat check girl in a Loop hotel and her shift was from eight-thirty on. She'd just have time to make it.

Honey and I had brandies and, since I'd run out of questions to ask her, she started asking them of me. I saw no reason not to tell her anything I'd learned to date, so I started with Nielson's phone call and went through my adventures of the day.

She looked at me a moment thoughtfully when I ran down, and smiled a bit mischievously. "Since you want to take a look at it, should we take a look together—at Albee's pad?"

"You mean you have a key?"

She was fumbling in her purse. "Pair of keys. Outer door and room. Just hadn't got around to throwing them away." She found them and handed them to me, two keys fastened together with a loose loop of string.

It was a real break, a chance to see Albee's pad and to have Honey see it with me. She'd be able to tell me how much of his stuff he'd taken, things like that. Besides, *I* could get in trouble using those keys by myself. But not if I was with Honey; if he'd

THE MISSING ACTOR

given her keys he'd given her the legal right to use them, whether he was there or not. Even Mrs. Radcliffe couldn't object to our going up there, not that we'd alert her if we could help it.

I bought us each a second brandy on the strength of those keys, then paid the tab and phoned for a taxi.

The landlady's door stayed closed when we passed it, and we didn't encounter anyone in the hallway or on the stairs. Albee's room, No. 9, was the front one on the third floor.

The moment I turned on the light and looked around I saw why Tom Chudakoff had called it a "padded pad." Except for a dresser there wasn't a piece of furniture in sight, but the floor was padded almost wall to wall. In one corner was a mattress with bedding and a pillow. The rest of the floor was scattered with green pads, the kind used on patio furniture. In all sizes. You could sit almost anywhere, fall almost anywhere. Real cool.

At the far end a curtain on a string masked what was no doubt the kitchenette, at one side there were two doors, one no doubt leading to a john and the other to a closet.

Honey closed the door and was looking around. She pointed to a bare area of floor on which there was a small stack of LP phonograph records. "His portable phono's gone. And part of his records. I'll check the closet."

She kicked off her shoes and started for one of the doors. I saw the point; it made sense to kick off your shoes in here. Then you could walk in a straight line; it didn't matter whether you stepped on floor or padding. Luckily, I was wearing loafers and I stepped out of them and followed her.

She was looking into a closet behind the door she'd opened and I looked over her shoulder. There were some clothes hanging there, but not many.

"There were two suitcases in here, and a lot more clothes. He cleared out, all right. With his phonograph and as many clothes as he could get into the two suitcases. I think he probably went to Los Angeles."

"Huh?" I said.

She pointed to one of the garments still in the closet. "His overcoat. He'd have taken that, even if he had to carry it over his arm, if he was going to New York. Or even San Francisco. It's an almost new overcoat; he just got it last winter."

"Why rule out Florida?" I asked.

"He told me he went there once and didn't like it. And that was Miami, the nearest thing there to a big city. And he didn't like the South, in general. Or Southerners, or Texans."

I tried the dresser while she looked into the bathroom and reported his shaving things were gone. The top three drawers of the dresser were empty. There was dirty linen in the bottom drawer; he hadn't had room for that. I ran my finger across the top of the dresser; there was at least a week's accumulation of dust.

"Doesn't seem to be any doubt he took off," I said.

Honey was disappearing behind the curtain that screened off the kitchenette. I wondered what she was looking for there. Not food, surely, after the big dinner we'd just eaten.

Then she pulled back the curtain part way and grinned at me, holding up a bottle. "Anyway, he left us half a bottle of Scotch."

"Going to take it along?"

"Not in the bottle," she said. "I'll find us glasses. Pick yourself a chair, man."

I laughed and picked myself a pad.

And jumped almost out of my clothes when a buzzer buzzed. Someone had just pushed the button under Albee's mailbox. I looked at Honey and she looked back, as startled as I was.

My first thought was to ignore it and then I realized that, as this was a front room, whoever was ringing would know that there was a light on, that someone was here.

I stood up quickly as it buzzed a second time. "I'll handle it," I told Honey. "Stay behind that curtain out of sight," I told her. I found the button beside the door that would release the catch

THE MISSING ACTOR

on the door downstairs and held it down a few seconds.

"If it's someone you know," I told Honey over my shoulder, "come on out. Otherwise stay there."

It was probably, I told myself, some casual friend of Albee's who, happening by, saw his light on. If that was the case, I could easily explain, identify myself, and get rid of him.

I stepped back into my loafers, for dignity, and waited.

When there was a knock on the door, I opened it.

I never really saw what he looked like. He stepped through the door the instant it opened and hit me once, with a fist like a piledriver, in the stomach. I hadn't been set for it, and it bent me over double and knocked the wind out of me, *all* the wind. I couldn't have spoken a word if my life depended upon it.

Luckily, it didn't. He could have swung a second time, to my chin, and knocked me cold and I wouldn't even have seen it coming. But he didn't. He stepped back and said, quite pleasantly, "Red would like you to drop up and see him. I think you better."

And he walked away. Honey was beside me by the time I could even start to straighten up. She was the one who closed the door. "Ed! Are you hurt?"

I couldn't talk to tell her that I couldn't talk and that that was a damn silly question anyway. She helped me to cross the room and to lie down on the mattress and she moved the pillow so it was under my head when I was able to straighten out enough to put my head down. She asked me if a drink would help and by that time I had enough breath back to tell her not yet, but if she wanted to help sooner than that she could hold my hand.

I'd been partly kidding, but she took me at my word, sat down on the edge of the mattress and held my hand. And maybe it did help; pretty soon I was breathing normally again and the acute phase of the pain had gone. I was going to have somewhat sore stomach muscles for several days.

What time I got home that night doesn't matter, but Uncle

Am was already asleep. He woke up, though, and wanted to know what gave, and I made with the highlights while I undressed. He frowned about the Kogan goon bit and wanted to know if I wanted to do anything about it. I said no, that obviously he hadn't known Albee by sight and had made a natural mistake under the circumstances, and that what I'd got was no more than Albee would have had coming.

I said, "I'll talk to this Jerry Score tomorrow, but I guess that'll wind it up, unless I get a lead from him. Up to now, the only thing that puzzles me is why old man Nielson still thinks there's a chance Albee didn't do what he obviously did do."

Uncle Am said, "Uh-huh. I didn't set the alarm, kid. I got to sleep early enough so I'll wake up in plenty of time. You sleep as late as you want to, since you can't see Score till afternoon."

I slept till ten. I was surprised when I got up to find a note from Uncle Am: "Ed, I've got a wild hunch that I want to get off my mind. I'm taking the car, and a run up to Kenosha. We won't bill our client for it unless it pays off. See you this evening if not sooner."

I puzzled about it a while and then decided to quit puzzling; I'd find out when Uncle Am got back. I took my time showering and dressing and left our room about eleven. I had a leisurely brunch and the morning paper and then it was noon. I phoned our office to see if by any chance Uncle Am was back or had phoned in; I got our answering service and learned there'd been no calls at all.

I went back to our room and read an hour and then it was time for me to leave if I wanted to get to the Graydon Theater at one-thirty. Rehearsal hadn't started yet, but Jerry Score was back and Carey Evers introduced us. He'd already explained about me to Score, so I didn't have to go through the routine.

He was a tall blond young man about my age or Albee's. Maybe just a touch on the swish side but not objectionably so.

And quite likeable and friendly. He gave me a firm handshake and suggested we go into the manager's office to talk. He wasn't in the first scene they'd be rehearsing and had plenty of time.

The manager's office contained only a battered desk, a file cabinet, and two chairs. He took one of the chairs and I sat on a corner of the desk.

His story matched what I'd learned from Honey and from everybody else. Yes, he was convinced Albee had taken a powder, and like Honey he was annoyed with Albee for not even having said so long before he took off.

I asked, "He didn't even give you a hint when he gave you back the car keys that Saturday night?"

"I didn't see him Saturday night. The last time I saw him was Saturday morning when he borrowed the car. He just dropped the keys into my mailbox when he brought it back."

I said, "But Lieutenant Chudakoff said that you said—" And then realized Tom hadn't said Score had *seen* Albee, just that Albee had returned the car keys.

I asked Score if he'd been home Saturday evening and he said yes, all evening. But that if I wondered why Albee had left the keys in the box instead of bringing them upstairs to him, the answer was simple. Since he'd decided to lam anyway he wanted to keep his get-away money intact, and he'd promised Jerry ten bucks for use of the car on the trip to Kenosha. If he'd seen him he'd have had to fork it over.

"The only thing that surprises me," Score said, "is that the old man came up with the money for him. Albee hadn't expected it, had made the Kenosha trip as a last desperate chance. I think now that he'd have blown town even without capital if the old man hadn't come through. With a sudden stake, he just couldn't resist it."

I asked if he knew what had happened at the bookstore and Score said sure, Albee had told him. He'd been managing to drag down about ten bucks a week besides his salary all the time he had worked there. Just tried to drag a bit too deeply that Friday morning because he was desperate about his bookie bill, and got caught with his hand in the till.

Score shrugged. "He'll land on his feet, wherever he went. He's — — — Ever see a picture of him?"

He got up and went to the file cabinet. "We got some stills here." He opened a drawer, hunted for and took out a file folder, handed me half a dozen eight-by-ten glossies, portrait shots. "Top one's straight, others made up for roles he played. One of 'em's as King Lear; that's the best role he ever played."

Albee was a good-looking young man all right, but what struck me was his resemblance to his father. It was really strong, one case where neither of them or anybody else could ever have denied the relationship. The second shot showed him as a mustachioed pirate with a black eye patch, as villainous a character as ever stormed a poop deck, whatever a poop deck is. The third — — —

The photographs shook a little in my hand. Albee as King Lear, with lines of age in his face and wild gray hair and a wild gray beard. He didn't look like his father in that shot; he *was* his father. Trim that beard. Instead of that gray wig, dye his own short hair. Let him talk like a Wisconsin farmer as, having known his father and being an actor, he certainly could do. . . .

I made the motions of looking at the rest of the glossies and handed them back. I thanked Jerry Score and made my get-away.

I walked south and walked blindly except when I had to cross a street without getting run over. Of course Floyd Nielson hadn't given away eight hundred dollars. Discount everything that Albee, as Floyd Nielson, had told us. Albee hadn't expected to get the loan and hadn't. But he'd learned his father had just sold the farm. Probably had all his money including the proceeds of the sale on hand, in cash. A fortune for a killing, whether it had been in cold blood or during a fight after a violent quarrel.

THE MISSING ACTOR

And then the fright and the planning. Establish that Albee had taken a powder, that his father was still alive and had gone west, where he'd gradually be lost track of. And if Albee showed up alive someday, somewhere, even came back to Chicago someday, so what? His father had been alive and looking for him long after Albee had gone. If his father's body were never found, there'd never have been a murder, never be an investigation.

And Uncle Am, even without having seen the photographs I'd just seen, had guessed it before I had. Or at least had seen it as a possibility. Right now he was on the Nielson farm, looking to see if there was a place where a body could have been put where it would never be found. Not a grave; a grave gives itself away by sinking unless there's someone around to keep it leveled off. But somewhere. . . .

If I'd had any sense I'd have gone to the office to wait for Uncle Am. Even if he hadn't found a body—and Albee could have disposed of it elsewhere than at the truck farm—we could prove a case, or let the cops prove it, just by pulling off Albee's beard; it was two inches long and he couldn't possibly have grown a real one in nine days.

But I didn't have any sense because I was walking into the lobby of the Ideal Hotel. A medium priced hotel, the kind the real Floyd Nielson would have chosen. Albee was staying in character and—suddenly I saw the reason why Albee Nielson had used first Missing Persons and then us as cats'-paws; he himself had *had* to stay away from even pretending to hunt for Albee on his own; Honey, Score, probably even his landlady, would have recognized him, gray beard or no. Which was why, too, he'd taken a hotel south of the Loop instead of on the Near North Side. In person, he'd avoided the area completely, except for his brief visit to our office.

I asked the clerk if Mr. Nielson was in. He glanced over his shoulder and said, "I guess so; his key's not in the box. Room two-fourteen."

There was an elevator, but I didn't wait for it; I walked up the stairs. I found 214 door and knocked on it. He opened it and said, "Oh, Mr. Hunter. Come in." I went in and he closed the door and looked at me. "Well, find out anything about Albee?"

And I realized then, too late, that I hadn't figured out what I was going to say or do. Give a tug on his beard? But I'd look, feel, and be too damn foolish if I was wrong, and I *could* be wrong.

I decided to toss out a feeler and see how he reacted to it.

I said, "The case isn't closed yet, Mr. Nielson. Something new has come up. There's a suspicion of murder."

And as suddenly as I'd been hit in the gut last night, I was being strangled. His hands were around my throat. There are people who fight by lashing out with their fists and there are stranglers. He was a strangler. And his hands were *strong*. Like a steel vise.

I tried to pull them away with my own hands and couldn't. Then, just in time, I remembered the trick for breaking a strangle hold taken from the front. You bring up your forearms inside his arms and jerk them apart. I tried it. It worked.

I took a step back quick while I had the chance, before he could grab me again. He didn't know boxing. He put up his guard too high and I swung a right in under it that got him in the gut just like the goon's swing last night got me. Maybe not as hard, but hard enough to bring his guard down. I feinted a left to keep them down and then put my right into his chin with all the weight of my body behind it, and he went down, out cold.

So cold that my first thought was to kneel beside him and make sure that his heart was still beating.

My second was the beard. It did *not* come off. And I bent down to study his face closely and saw that the age lines in it were etched and not drawn.

I sat down on the edge of the bed and stayed sitting there for about nine hours. Anyway, it seemed that long. I gently massaged

THE MISSING ACTOR 195

my neck where those strong hands had gripped it, and then I looked down at those strong hands and wondered how I could have been so blind as not to notice them the first time we'd talked to him. They were, even aside from their own indications of age, the muscled, hard, callused hands of a farmer, not the hands of a book-store clerk. Uncle Am had always told me to look at people's hands as well as their faces when I was sizing them up. I hadn't even noticed Floyd Nielson's hands.

He began to stir, and his eyes opened.

And there were footsteps in the hallway outside and a heavy knock on the door, a cop's kind of knock. I called out, "Come in!"

The first one through was a cop I knew slightly, Lieutenant Guthrie of Homicide. The second man I didn't know; I later learned he was a Kenosha County Sheriff's deputy. The third man in was Uncle Am.

Nielson sat up.

Guthrie said, "Floyd Nielson, you are under arrest for suspicion of the murder of Albee Nielson. Anything-you-say-may-be-used-against-you." He produced a pair of handcuffs.

Uncle Am winked at me. "Come on, kid. They won't need us, not now anyway. We may have to testify later."

I went with him. Outside he said, "You beat me to him, Ed, but damn it, you shouldn't have tackled him alone."

I said, "Yeah."

"There's a likely looking bar across the street. I think we've earned a drink. How's about it?"

"Yeah," I said.

We ordered drinks. Uncle Am said, "You gave me the idea, kid, when you said, last thing last night, that what puzzled you was that he wouldn't just accept that Albee had taken it on the lam, go on to California and wait to hear from Albee if Albee ever chose to write. What he did was out of character, spending a full week in Chicago heckling first Missing Persons and then us. He just wanted it firmly established that Albee *had* taken a powder."

"Yeah," I said.

"With the hypothetical money. It would have been out of character for him to give Albee that money to begin with, and he didn't. So they got into a fight over it and he killed Albee. That's my guess, and if it was that, he could probably have got away with self-defense if he'd called the sheriff right away. But he wanted to play it cute."

"Yeah," I said.

"So I guessed he'd have disposed of the body on the farm rather than risk moving it, so I went there. I looked around with the idea of where I'd put a body where it never would be found unless someone looked for it. A grave in the open was out. But there was a brand new cement floor in the tool shed. The new owner was surprised Nielson had gone to that trouble after he'd already sold the farm. So I called the sheriff and he brought men with picks."

"Yeah," I said.

"One thing puzzles me. How he got Albee to take Jerry's car back to him and then return to the farm to be killed. That part doesn't make sense."

I said, "He brought the car back to Chicago himself Saturday evening, left it in front of Jerry's and left the keys in Jerry's mail box. He had the address on the car registration."

"And then went back to Kenosha by bus or however, got his pickup truck and came to Chicago again to use Albee's keys to raid his pad in the middle of the night. Sure. There were two suitcases and a portable phonograph under that cement, besides Albee. Well, kid, however *you* figured it out, you beat me to the answer."

I said, "Uncle Am, I cannot tell a lie."

"What the hell do you mean?"

THE MISSING ACTOR

"I mean it's four o'clock. Let's knock off as of now and have a night on the town. We're due for one anyway."

"Sure, kid, we're overdue. But what's that got to do with your not being able to tell a lie?"

I said, "I mean I need two more drinks before I can tell you the truth."

"Then let's have them right here and get it over with. Okay?"

"Okay," I said.

And we ordered our second round, and then our third.